It was a ludicrous paradox. The bow and arrow is among the most ancient and primitive of weapons. This one, though, was a shining testament to modern technology: all metal and fiberglass, a thin steel cable instead of a string, pulleys, weights and counterweights, even a telescopic sight. The hands that held this sleek and awesome instrument of destruction and nocked the hunting arrow with its four lethal steel blades were gloved in thin black leather. He stood there for an instant, seemingly frozen in time, the bow held by pressure alone against his open left hand, the drunken man in the cabin clearly visible in the sight through the open door.

The fool, he thought. *He's making it so easy.*

He inhaled deeply, steadied his arm, and began to expel his breath slowly as he relaxed his two crooked fingers to allow the steel cable to slip free, sending the deadly missile hurtling with incredible velocity through the open cabin door.

◄ ►

Wilder & Wilder

Wilder
&
Wilder

ROBERT J. CONLEY

PAGEANT BOOKS

Publisher's Note: This is a work of fiction. The characters, incidents, and dialogues are products of the author's imagination and are not to be construed as real. Any resemblance to actual events or persons, living or dead, is entirely coincidental.

PAGEANT BOOKS
225 Park Avenue South
New York, New York 10003

Cover artwork by Isa Barnett

Printed in the U.S.A.

First Pageant Books printing: November, 1988

10 9 8 7 6 5 4 3 2 1

for Clu and Miriam

special thanks to Kenny Graham
and Don Keeler

Wilder
&
Wilder

Chapter One

THEY SAY THE grass is always greener on the other side of the fence. That must have been what Ajax was thinking. He stood on the inside of the stretched hog wire just beside the road not far from the mailbox. If he turned his head to just the right angle, he knew, from past experience, that he could shove his head through the lower openings. He twisted his head and eased it forward. His beard stroked the lower wire and his horns scraped the tiny wire knots at the corners of the square. Stretching his neck, he began to nibble at the tips of the tall grass that grew along the side of the road. It wasn't long, however, before Ajax had devoured all he wanted of what he could reach. He knew, also from past experience, what would come next. He knew that, trying to back out of the hole he had put himself in, the backward sweep of his horns would prevent his escape. He was trapped, and he knew it, but he tried anyway. He backed up. The tips of his horns caught on the wire. He pulled. Then he began to call for help.

About sixty yards up a long, unpaved, rocky driveway, wet and puddled from one of those surprise thunderstorms so common in northeastern Oklahoma, inside a modest three-bedroom house, Jackson Wilder was sitting at the kitchen table sipping coffee from a cup and reading from a small stack of typed sheets of paper. His wife, Margaret, had just pushed the plunger down to lower two slices of whole wheat bread into the toaster and was rushing to the refrigerator when they heard the familiar bleat coming from the direction of the road. Margaret stopped in the middle of the floor and cast a quick glance toward the front door.

"Oh," she said, "that's Ajax."

Jackson had already put down his cup. With obvious but mild irritation, he tossed the papers down onto the table, put both hands down on the table edge and leaned back with a sigh, looking toward the ceiling.

"That damn goat," he said.

"Well, he's stuck in the fence again, Jack," said Margaret on her way to the table with the butter. "Go help him out."

"You'd think he'd learn after a while. You'd think he would have picked up some horse sense by now."

"He's a goat," said Margaret.

Jackson got up slowly from the table and headed for the picture window by the front door in the living room. He pushed the drawn drapes aside with the back of his hand, trying to look sideways down the drive to see where the goat was calling from. He couldn't see him from the window.

"Hot damn," he said.

He went down the hallway to the bedroom and sat on the edge of the bed to pull on a pair of low quarter tennis shoes, then he picked a blue chambray work shirt off a hook in the closet and pulled it on. Not bothering to button the shirt, he headed back through the house to the front door. On the way out, he picked his battered Stetson off a hat tree in the living room.

"He just wants attention," said Margaret, already running around the kitchen again. "He wants you to come out and see him."

"Yeah," said Jackson, opening the front door. "Well, I think it's about time we had us some goatburgers around here. That's what I think. Dammit."

As he slammed the door behind himself, his wife called out after him just as the toast popped up and she was grabbing for it.

"Don't talk like that about Ajax. He's just a pet. He loves you."

She reached for a butter knife, and, though she knew that Jackson was beyond her hearing, she had more to say. She didn't bother yelling it out anymore. She just talked as if he were in the room with her.

"And you love him, too. You just like to talk that way. You wouldn't anymore eat burgers made out of Ajax than I would."

*   *   *

Jackson picked his way down the long puddle-spotted driveway, breathing in the fresh scent of the early-morning, after-storm air. When he arrived at the end of the driveway, the mailbox on a post to his right, the corner to his left fenced, he looked to his left and found Ajax. The goat was standing inside the fence with his head poked through out toward the road.

"Oh, dammit, Ajax, dammit," said Jackson, mashing the fence down so he could step over it. He walked through the tall, wet grass a few steps to stand beside the captive goat, his hands on his hips. He cocked his head and stared at the forlorn-looking prisoner.

"You thick-skulled, silly old bastard," he said. "What the hell are you going to do now?"

Ajax's head was ducked by necessity, and he rolled his eyes up toward Jackson. Then he emitted a pleading bleat.

"What would you do if you got stuck like this and nobody was home, huh?"

The goat rolled its eyes.

"What if I was gone off on a vacation or something? Gone for two weeks or a month? You'd starve to death out here like this."

Jackson squatted down beside the wretched goat and stroked its back.

"I'd come home and find your old worthless bones hanging on the wire. Maybe your old hide still stretched over them. Damn. You got ticks all over you, boy."

Jackson pulled a fat, gray tick loose from Ajax's ribcage and tossed it over the fence and out into the road.

"We'll have to get you cleaned up here in a bit."

Ajax gave another bleat.

"All right. All right."

Jackson reached through the wires to get hold of the goat's horns.

"Can't even let me finish a cup of coffee in the morning, can you?" he said. "Here. Here. Turn your head. Come on."

As he twisted the goat's head to allow the animal to pull back through the fence and free himself, Jackson heard a car coming down the rocky dirt road.

"There you go, you big baby," he said, as Ajax frisked, enjoying his freedom. "Mailman's coming."

Jackson watched down the road until he saw the mail car loom up over the rise. It pulled up and stopped beside the fence.

"Morning, Jack," said the driver.

"Howdy, Homer. What you got there for me this morning? Bunch of junk mail? That's what it usually is. Junk mail."

Homer held a stack of mail in his hands and slowly thumbed through it.

"Oh, let's see here," he said. "Bills, mostly. Looks like a check from your publisher here. *TV Guide.* And here's a letter from your agent."

"Well, hell, let me have it, will you? Or you going to open it and read it to me?"

Homer handed the mail out the window of his car and stretched his arm to hand it across the fence to Jackson, who took it and quickly shuffled past the bills to the two significant items mentioned by Homer.

"I just finished your latest," said Homer. *"Six-gun Range*. Hell of a good book. I'll bring it around for you to sign."

"Yeah. You do that, Homer. Anytime. When are you going to read one of Maggie's books?"

Homer took off his Kansas City Royals baseball cap and scratched the top of his head.

"Oh, I can't get into those mysteries," he said. "Give me a good western anytime. The wife reads them, though."

"Why don't you two swap books? Broaden your reading a little?"

"Naw," said Homer, shifting the mail car into low gear, "she wouldn't touch one of yours, except maybe with a cattle prod. See you around."

Jackson chuckled to himself as Homer drove on down the road. Then, feeling a tug, he looked down to see Ajax eating at his shirttail. He pulled the shirt loose from the goat's teeth and shoved the animal's head away from him.

"Damn you, Ajax," he said. "Look at all this tall grass. Look at it. What the hell you want to eat my shirt for? It just rained. The grass is wet and juicy. And what do you want to stick your head through the damn fence for? There's nothing wrong with this grass right here except that you've let it grow too high. If you don't keep the grass down for me, what good are you? Why do you think I keep you anyway?"

While he was talking to the goat, Jackson had climbed back over the fence. He trotted the distance back to the house, jumping over puddles. Jerking open the front door, he called out to Maggie.

"Got a check here, babe."

"Oh, good," said Maggie. "Bring it on in here. I've just about got our breakfast ready. What else is there?"

"Bills, bills, bills," said Jackson, sitting down at the table and dropping envelopes in front of him. "Got to have bills if you get a check. Got to have some place for that check to go."

"Oh, I know it. Here, let me pour you a fresh cup of coffee. That one's got cold while you were out. How's Ajax?"

"Ajax. I should have left him hung up in the fence. Blockhead. Got a letter from Tom here."

"Oh. What does Tom have to say?"

"Well, I don't know," said Jackson, tearing open the envelope. "I haven't read it yet. Let's see here. It looks like a form letter. It's got our names typed in the greeting, but it looks like a form letter."

"Well, read it," said Maggie.

"Says, 'Dear Jack and Maggie, I hope you'll excuse this form letter—' See there. I told you it looked like a form letter."

"Oh, Jack, read the letter, will you?"

She put a fresh cup of coffee in front of him and scurried back across the room to the stove to stir the sausage gravy one last time.

"Says, 'Dear Jack and Maggie, I hope you'll excuse this form letter, but I have the same thing to write to all my favorite clients. This has been a particularly successful year for the Brock Agency. We have sold more books this year than in any two years in the past, and that success is due to you. I have decided that this calls for a celebration, and I'm inviting all of you to join me at the expense of the agency for five days at the Hunter Dude Ranch in Wyoming. We'll have a great time. A brochure describing the ranch is enclosed, and I'm instructing my secretary to make travel arrangements for you all. Your airline tickets will be waiting for you at your nearest airport, prepaid and in your own name. Also enclosed is an itinerary sheet with all dates and times. You will be picked up at the other end by the Hunter Ranch van and driven to the ranch. I'm assuming you will all attend unless I hear otherwise from you. Don't disappoint me. This is a special occasion. Very sincerely yours, Tom Brock.'"

Maggie rushed over to the table and took the letter out of Jackson's hands.

"A dude ranch," she exclaimed.

"Yeah."

"Oh, that sounds like fun. We're going, aren't we?"

"Hell, as long as it's on Tom, we might as well. Got to keep Tom happy as long as he sells our books."

"Oh, Jack. I think this is real nice of Tom. Don't you?"

"Yeah, it really is," he said. "I'll have to go over and talk to Sherman. Get him to watch out for the place while we're gone. Keep the goat out of the fence and what not."

"Yes. Yes. Sherman will do that for us, won't he?"

"Sure he will. Say, here's a brochure on the ranch. Another one on Wyoming."

"Oh, let me see."

"Ajax has ticks all over him. All over him."

"We'd better get them off of him. You need to

go into the feed store and get him a collar. And get a bag of that stuff. You know."

"That tick stuff. I know."

"Yeah. That stuff you spread all over the ground to kill ticks."

"Well, I'll do that here in a while. I'll go see Sherman, and I'll go into town and get that stuff. You want to go in?"

"No. I have too much to do here. I'll stay home."

"Okay. Say. Do I get to eat this morning?"

Jackson Wilder had finished his breakfast and brushed his teeth. He climbed into his dusty old Ford pickup and turned the key. The starter whirred for a moment before the engine fired up, and Jackson revved it a few times, then shoved it into reverse and backed around in the yard to get it aimed head first down the long, bumpy driveway. He took off, splashing through the puddles. As he turned the corner by the mailbox to get out onto the road, he stuck his head out the window and yelled at Ajax.

"Keep out of the fence, knothead."

Maggie had just finished cleaning up the kitchen after breakfast, and for the first time since she had gotten out of bed, she slowed down her pace. She sat down at the kitchen table to look at the material that had accompanied Tom Brock's letter. She had been too busy moving about, doing this and that, to have really taken it in while Jackson had read through it earlier. With Jack gone to visit their neighbor, Sherman Postoak, she would have a little time to herself. She looked at the itinerary Tom had enclosed. It gave her a date to be at the Hunter Ranch.

"Oh," she said to herself, "that's just a few days."

It also gave her a date, time and flight number for their flight to Sheridan, Wyoming. With their tickets already reserved and paid for, and arrangements for a van from the ranch to drive them out, there was really nothing left for Jackson and Maggie to do, except pack and prepare their home for their absence. Jackson had gone to see Sherman about watching over things. They would have to tell Homer to hold their mail. Either that or Sherman could bring it into the house each day. She'd wait and see whether or not Jack had asked him to do that. Maggie put down the itinerary and picked up the colorful brochure from the Hunter Dude Ranch. There were color pictures of the mountains, pictures of the buildings on the ranch, of cowboys at work, of a chuckwagon out on the range. Maggie thought that it would all be very exciting. Suddenly she jumped up from her chair.

"Oh," she said, "I've got to get our clothes ready."

Driving toward Sherman Postoak's house, Jackson was thinking about the trip, too, but his thoughts were on Drago. Robert Drago was another of Tom Brock's clients, and at one time, Robert and his wife, Sylvia, had been just about the best friends of Jackson and Maggie. It would be nice to see Robert again. It had been about seven years, Jackson guessed. When Drago's books had begun to sell, he and Sylvia had packed up and moved to New York City. They would be closer to Bob's publishers and to his agent, they had said. They had tried to talk Jack and Maggie into doing the same thing for the same reasons, but Jack wouldn't think of leaving Oklahoma. "I've got a good mailman," he had said, and Maggie had agreed with him. In New York City they would have no place to keep their animals. The Wilders and the Dragos had kept up a correspondence for a while, but when the Dragos separated and then divorced, even that had stopped. Yeah, Jackson thought, it would be nice to see Robert again. He hoped that Drago would accept Brock's offer and be at the Dude Ranch.

He turned the pickup into Sherman Postoak's drive, shoved it into second and roared down toward the house, spraying mud and dirty water behind him. As he approached the house, he saw Sherman standing off to one side. Sherman had just put one end of a four-foot-long cane pole to his lips. He took a deep breath, then blew it out through the pole in a quick puff. A six-inch locust wood dart tufted with bull thistledown thunked into a homemade paper target tacked onto a stack of hay bales about twenty-five or thirty feet away. Sherman lowered the pole and turned to face his visitor.

" '*Siyo*, Jack," he said. "What brings you over this way?"

Jackson turned off the engine and stepped out of the Ford, watching for the mudholes.

" '*Siyo*, buddy. What the hell are you up to there?"

"Getting ready for the big contest," said Sherman.

He held up the cane pole for Jackson to see. It was decorated with painted designs and with rawhide strips. At one point a small bunch of fringe dangled, and at just about the center of the pole were tied two short pheasant feathers. Extra darts were tucked into the rawhide strip that was wrapped around the pole at the center, the same strip from which the feathers depended. Jack took the pole in his hands.

"Oh yeah," he said. "I'd forgot about that. Big blowgun contest coming up soon at the Cherokee holiday. You going to win it this year are you?"

"I don't know," said Sherman, wrinkling his brow and looking studious. "I might have a pretty fair chance if it's just us young guys that enters, you know? But if the old-timers gets in on it—boy, they're good."

Jackson chuckled out loud. He was fifty-five years old and knew that Sherman was at least a couple of years older than that. He extended his arm to hand the blowgun back to Sherman, but Sherman didn't take it.

"Try it out."

"Well," said Jack, and he carefully removed a dart from the rawhide strip. He poked the dart into the end of the blowgun, then raised the end to his mouth.

"Take a deep breath," said Sherman.

Jack filled his lungs with air, aimed the gun and expelled the air at once. The dart tore the edge of the paper target as it buried itself in the hay.

"Boy, that's wicked," he said, handing the blowgun back to Sherman. Sherman took it and walked over to his old GMC pickup to toss it in on the seat.

"So," he said, "like I said before, what brings you over?"

"Ah," said Jack, "I got a shindig to go to up in Wyoming for a few days. Agent's throwing a big bash for us big shot writers at a dude ranch up there."

Postoak grinned.

"A dude ranch?" he said. "Is that any kind of place for an Oklahoma Indian boy to go to? A dude ranch?"

He shook his head as if to express disapproval of the whole idea.

"Well, you know, the man pays the bills. Besides that, you're one of the few people around who calls me Indian. Hell, I'm a half-assed Indian and a drugstore cowboy. That dude ranch is probably just the place for me. I might get up there and stay. You never can tell."

"So what do you need? You want me to watch the place while you're gone? Keep the white men off? The white man sure does like to get his hands on that Indian land. You and me still got our old family allotments. I want to protect that Indian land. I'll watch it for you. Don't worry."

"Thanks, Sherm. I knew you would."

"You don't come back from that dude ranch, I'll just move some of my kids in your house, that's all."

"Yeah, well, I guess that'd be all right, if I don't come back."

"Come over and sit down on the porch with

me," said Sherman, "and let's have a smoke. One of yours."

Jackson turned to follow Sherman to the porch. The house was small and simple, even compared to Jackson's modest home, but it was well put together and always kept clean. There were no chairs on the porch. They sat on the rough boards. Jackson felt of his shirt pockets as if he were searching for a cigarette pack.

"I don't have any," he said. "Hell, you know I don't smoke. I never carry smokes."

"I guess we'll have to smoke mine, then," said Sherman, pulling a pack out of his shirt pocket and offering it to Jackson.

Jackson took a cigarette out of the pack and lit it. He drew deeply on it, then exhaled the smoke. It was true that he didn't smoke. Not regularly. But now and then, when a cigarette was offered to him and he took it, he had to admit that it was good.

"Written any more good books lately?" asked Sherman, the curls of white smoke drifting slowly out of his mouth and nostrils and offering a contrast to his dark skin.

"Naw. Not since the last one you read. Hell, I can't write them fast enough to keep up with you."

"Well, let me know. I'm ready for another one."

"Yeah. I'll do that. I've got some good westerns at home written by some of my friends. I'll loan you a few of them to read."

"Nope," said Sherman. "I don't know them guys."

"They're good writers."

"Yonegs?" said Sherman.

"Yeah. Yeah," said Jack. "They're white men."

Jackson took another long drag on the cigarette. It was beginning to make him slightly lightheaded.

"Do you ever read anything besides my books?" he asked.

"Yeah. I read Maggie's."

"Maggie's a white woman," said Jack.

"Maggie's different."

"Anything else?"

"Just my Cherokee Bible."

Jackson shook his head and smiled.

"Say, Sherm," he said, "I'm worried about that damn goat of mine."

"Which one?"

"Ajax."

"Oh, Ajax," said Sherm.

"Yeah. I had to get his damn head out of the fence again this morning. I'm afraid that he'll stick his neck through there while I'm gone and starve himself to death."

"Well, you just go on to that dude ranch and have yourself a good time. I'll watch out after old Ajax better than you can."

"Oh, my God," said Maggie, "we'll miss our plane."

The tires on the pickup squealed as Jackson spun into the airport's long-term parking lot.

"Just calm down," he said. "We've got plenty of time. Trust me."

"But I'm so nervous. We're running late and I like to be on time. Really, I'd like to be early if we could, just for once."

"Trust me. We're not going to miss the flight. We've already got our tickets, and you don't need to get here so early when you've already got your tickets."

"Watch out for that car."

Jackson swerved and almost hit a parked Cadillac. He'd have been all right had Maggie not said anything. His swerving was a reaction to her warning, not to anything real in his path.

"Maggie," he said, as he straightened up the pickup and headed for a parking slot he'd spied up ahead, "you make me nervous, but I love you."

Jackson locked the doors of the pickup in spite of the fact that the window wing on the passenger's side was broken out and anyone could reach in to open the door.

"You trot on ahead and get our tickets, babe," he said. He reached into the bed of the pickup for the bags as Maggie sped through the lot, her red hair streaming behind her. He followed as fast as he could, but the bags were heavy. By the time Jackson had struggled through the lot and across the street to the main terminal, Maggie was waving frantically at him through a crowd on the sidewalk.

"Right here," she said. "Right here."

"What do you mean? What is this? Do you have the tickets?"

"I got the tickets, but they're checking bags right out here."

"You check the bags at the counter where you get the tickets," said Jackson.

"You can," said Maggie, "but you can do it

here if you already have your tickets. It's three dollars a bag either way."

"What?"

"It's part of some economy thing or something. The tickets are cheaper but there's no service whatsoever. You pay for everything. Here. Here's the man."

Jackson shelled out twelve dollars for the four bags he had been lugging, and Maggie grabbed him by the arm.

"Hell of a note," he said.

"Come on," she said. "They're already boarding."

"We'll make it," said Jackson, but he ran to keep Maggie from pulling him awkwardly along behind her. They raced up the steps and into the terminal, charged down the hallway and jumped on the escalator. Maggie wasn't content to just ride. Still clutching Jackson by his arm, she charged up the moving steps until she found their path blocked by a portly couple who were quite content to lounge their way to the top. Maggie's frustration with the unwelcome obstacle was obvious. At the top of the escalator they raced again down the hallway. At the end of the long corridor, Maggie turned loose of Jack's arm long enough to dash through the doorframe at the security check point. A buzzer sounded and a big guard stepped in front of her.

"Hold on," he said. "Go back through there and put that bag on the counter."

"Oh," said Maggie, turning to go back through the doorframe. "Oh, I'm sorry. I'm just in such a hurry that I forgot."

She deposited her handbag on the counter so

that it could ride through the X-ray tunnel, then she walked back through the doorframe.

"I really wasn't trying to slip anything through on you," she said. "It's just that we're running so late. I'm sorry."

The guard picked up Maggie's handbag as it emerged from the safe end of the tunnel and handed it to her. He didn't say a word, and she turned to hurry on down the hallway to the proper departure gate. Confused, she turned to check on Jackson. He stepped through the doorway and the buzzer sounded.

"Back through," said the guard.

Jackson stepped back through. He felt of his pockets. The guard shoved a basket toward him. Jackson emptied his pockets of change, a penknife and nail clippers. Then he stepped back through the doorway. The buzzer sounded again.

"Damn," he said.

He pulled the watch off his wrist and tossed it into the basket, then felt his pockets again.

"Oh."

He pulled a ring off his finger and threw that into the basket.

"What else? What else?" he said. "Let's see here. Oh, hell yes. I know what it is."

He reached down to unfasten his belt and pull off the heavy metal buckle stamped with the great seal of the Cherokee Nation of Oklahoma. He tossed the buckle into the basket and walked through the doorframe again. This time he made it without setting off the buzzer. Smugly, he reached for the basket and poured all of its contents into the side pocket of his sports jacket.

"Come on," said Maggie.

"I'm coming. Don't worry. We'll make it. Which gate?"

"Right down here," said Maggie, dragging him along beside her.

They sat sweating on the plane for fifteen minutes while airline officials checked out some minor malfunction before they finally took to the air.

"What'd I tell you?" said Jackson. "I told you they wouldn't leave without us. They must know who we are, you reckon? Couple of big writers? Maybe they'll come by and ask for our autographs. Ask us to sign a couple of books."

The stewardess leaned down toward Jackson, a friendly smile pasted on her heavily made up face.

"Can I get you something to drink?" she asked.

"Yeah," he said. "I'd like a cup of coffee. Just black coffee."

"That will be one dollar, please," said the stewardess through the unmoving smile.

"A dollar," said Jackson, just a little loud. Maggie gouged him in the side with her elbow and leaned over to whisper harshly in his ear.

"It's the economy flight," she said. "No service."

Jackson pulled out a dollar bill for the coffee.

"God damn that Brock anyway," he said. "You want anything, babe?"

Chapter Two

THE ARRIVAL AT the Sheridan airport was easy and comfortable compared to the Tulsa departure. Even getting the bags was no problem. Jackson carried the heaviest bags, with Maggie following with the two lightest ones. They made their way outside to the curb where limousines and taxicabs awaited riders.

"There's a van over there," said Maggie.

Jackson squinted in the hot Wyoming sun.

"Naw," he said, "that's a hotel van."

"Well," said Maggie, "all the vans that I can see are hotel vans. Tom said that there would be a van here to pick us up. He said a Hunter Ranch van. I remember that's what the letter said."

"Yeah, well, I'm sure there will be. Don't worry. Hey, wait a minute. Look over there."

"Where?"

"That jeep over there with the cowboy in it," said Jackson. "Look. Can you read that?"

"Yes," said Maggie, "it says, 'Hunter Ranch.' Tom said it would be a van."

"I know. I know," said Jackson. "Let's just go have a word with the cowboy. What do you say?"

Not waiting for an answer, Jackson hefted his two bags and headed for the jeep. Maggie hustled along behind.

"Say, buddy. Excuse me," said Jackson.

The cowboy in the jeep turned his head.

"Are you Mr. Wilder?" he said.

Just then Maggie came running up to stand

beside Jackson. The cowboy jumped out of the jeep and took off his hat. A broad smile swept across his face.

"Well," he said, "sure you are. I recognize Mrs. Wilder here from the pictures on the dust jackets of her books. My name's Monte Clark, Mrs. Wilder. I'm real pleased to meet you. I've read most all of your books."

"How about mine?" asked Jackson.

"Oh," said Monte, turning to Jackson, "pleased to meet you, too, sir. No, I can't say as I have. I don't read westerns. I sure do like your wife's mystery novels, though. I buy them all in hardcover. Don't wait for them to come out in paper. Maybe I could get you to sign them for me while you're here at the ranch."

"I'd be happy to," said Maggie. "Thank you."

"I take it," said Jackson, getting irritated with the conversation, "that you're our ride out to the ranch."

"Yes, sir, that's right."

Monte Clark took the bags out of Maggie's hands and tossed them into the jeep. Jackson hefted the two heavy ones in after them.

"It was supposed to be a van," said Maggie. "We were looking for a van."

"Oh," said Clark, the grin still on his face, "the van didn't come in because there's just the two of you."

"Just the two of us?" said Jack. "There should be a bunch of us. Tom Brock invited a whole group of his clients."

"Oh, they're all out at the ranch, all right," said the cowboy as he climbed back into the jeep behind the wheel. "You two are just the last ones to arrive is what I meant. The others are all out there already. Well, hop in. We got a bit of a ride ahead of us."

Maggie got into the front passenger seat and Jackson climbed into the rear with a groan. Just as he sat back, Monte Clark popped the clutch and the jeep took off, throwing Jack against the seat back. Soon they were out on the highway.

"Say, buddy," shouted Jackson, his voice competing with the combined high-pitched whine of the jeep's engine and the roar of the wind, "do you punch cows or just herd dudes around?"

"A little bit of both," shouted Clark over his shoulder. "Dude ranch season is just in the summer. The rest of the year we're a regular working cattle ranch."

"It sounds exciting," said Maggie.

"It's all right," said Clark, then with another glance over his shoulder, he added, "You ranch?"

"Naw," said Jackson, "I'm a writer. What made you ask that?"

"The way you're dressed. I thought maybe you were a cowboy down there in Oklahoma. Don't they have ranches in Oklahoma?"

"Yeah, sure, we have them," said Jackson, glancing down at his faded jeans and beat-up boots. "We have ranches, but me, I've just got a few acres. Couple of horses to ride. A few goats."

Jackson wondered whether or not Ajax was hung up in the fence, and if so, how long it would be before Sherman Postoak got around to checking up on him.

"They're really just pets," said Maggie.

"A goat roper, huh?" said Clark.

Jackson thought that it would be interesting to

catch Monte Clark by the nape of his neck and toss him out of the moving jeep into the ditch alongside the road. *Little snit*, he thought.

"Not even that, buddy," he said. "Not even that."

"Oh, look," shouted Maggie, turning in her seat and pointing off to the right side of the jeep into an expanse of Wyoming's open range. "What are they?"

Jackson shouted out his answer, a little too quickly, he thought, but he was determined to get it out before the smart-mouthed cowboy had a chance to show off any more.

"Antelope, babe," he said. "Those are antelope."

"They're beautiful."

"Lot of them up here," said Clark. "Last season I bagged me a real beaut. Big buck."

"Oh," said Maggie.

"Shot the poor bastard, did you?" said Jack. "What kind of cannon you use?"

"Got me a M-1 Garrand," said Clark. "It's one of the International Harvesters. Real rare. You know, most of them's Springfields. Yep. International Harvester stamped right on the barrel. That's a damn fine rifle. Uncle Sam knows what he's doing when he buys weapons. Yes, sir."

Jackson thought of a half dozen things to say to Monte Clark about his Uncle Sam and his International Harvester rifle, but instead he settled back into the jeep's small back seat for the duration of the ride. There was no sense in allowing the young cowboy to irritate him, and if he sat back, he wouldn't be able to hear anything that was said in the front seats for the roar of the wind, the high pitched whine of the engine and the loud and monotonous drone of the over-sized, knobby tires on the hot pavement. Soon Monte Clark turned the jeep off the highway and drove it under a large wooden sign that was hanging between two tall posts. The sign read: HUNTER RANCH.

"Here we are," he shouted.

"Yeah, I can see that," said Jackson. "My mother taught me to read before I even started school. I could read when I was four years old."

"Hey, that's not bad," said Clark. "Four years old, huh?"

It was about a mile down the driveway before they came to the ranch buildings. The nearest was a large, modern house made of logs. Then a row of small cabins ran on down the road from that. Clark pulled the jeep to a stop and put it in neutral.

"This here's the lodge," he said, indicating the largest building. "That's probably where everybody else is at right now. There's a bar in there. Barbecue scheduled out back in about an hour or so. You can get out here and say howdy to everyone, or I can take you on over to your cabin."

"How far's the cabin?" said Jackson.

The cowboy pointed to the row of small log cabins, all within easy walking distance of the lodge.

"Right there," he said. "Fifth one down. It's got a shower and everything, in case you want to freshen up before you eat. See the jeep parked outside?"

It appeared to be just like the one they were in

except that it had a different number painted on the door, and it was parked just outside the front door to the cabin.

"Yeah," said Jackson.

"Well, it's yours as long as you're guests here. The keys are in it."

"I think we'd better go on down to the cabin," said Jackson. "What do you say, Maggie?"

"Yes, I need to freshen up before I meet anyone. I'm so anxious to see everybody, but I'd better freshen up first."

"Yeah, why don't you run us down there?"

"You're the boss," said Monte Clark, popping the clutch and flinging gravel behind them as the jeep lurched forward.

At the cabin, Clark helped Jackson unload the luggage, showed him the key in the door and reminded him of the key to the jeep in its ignition.

"Anything else you folks need?" he asked.

"No," said Jackson. "No. I think we're all right here. Thank you."

He was reaching into his wallet for a few bills.

"Hey," said Clark, holding up a hand. "No tips. It's all part of the service. Let me know if you need anything."

He tipped his hat to Maggie and went out to the jeep, driving off in a cloud of dust. Jackson shoved his wallet back into his pocket.

"He's a nice young man," said Maggie. "Don't you think he's nice, Jack?"

"Yeah," said Jack. "The little dodo."

"What?"

"I said, 'Yeah, he's a nice young fella.' Yeah."

*   *   *

Tom Brock jumped up from the chair in which he sat between two lovely young ladies, leaving his drink on the table in front of him. He held his arms out wide and rushed toward the door of the lounge, known as The Old Corral, inside the Hunter Ranch Lodge.

"Jackson," he shouted. "Maggie. God, it's good to see you. I thought you'd never get here."

By the time he had finished his last sentence, Brock had made his way across the room to where Jackson and Maggie Wilder had just stepped inside the door, and he had thrown his arms around both of them. Maggie put an arm around Brock's back and hugged him. Her other arm was pinned between Brock and Jackson. Jackson was embarrassed by public hugging. He raised his one free arm in a half-hearted gesture and tentatively patted Brock's shoulder.

"How are you, Tom?" he said.

"Oh, I'm great. Doing great. Couldn't be better."

Brock turned his victims loose and backed up a step to look at them.

"Gee, it's good to see you," he said.

"Yeah," said Jackson. "Yeah. You said that. It's good to see you, Tom."

He extended his hand for Brock to shake, a greeting much more comfortable to him than hugging. Brock took his hand and covered the handshake with his left. Jackson thought that Brock could find a way to turn anything into a hug.

"How was the trip?" asked Brock. "Okay?"

"Yeah," said Jackson. "It was fine. Just fine."

"Oh, God," said Maggie. "We almost missed the flight in Tulsa, and then we had to pay extra to check our bags. I thought that Jack was never going to get through airport security. And then . . ."

"Maggie," said Jackson. "It was fine, Tom. Uneventful. The best kind of trip."

"Good," said Brock, putting an arm around the shoulders of both Jack and Maggie and leading them toward the table where his drink waited for him. "Good. Come on over and say hello to the others. This is my secretary, Myrna Keck. I don't think you guys have ever met before, have you?"

"No," said Jack. "No, we haven't."

"Myrna, this is Jack and Maggie Wilder."

"Oh," said Myrna, turning in her chair and extending a limp hand, "I've heard so much about you. I'm very glad to meet you. You know, this is all very exciting for me. I've only been working for Tom for about six weeks, and it's really exciting to be meeting all these writers. Gee, now that I know you I'll have to read some of your books."

"Yeah," said Jack. "You do that."

"It's nice meeting you, Myrna," said Maggie.

Brock had put a hand on the shoulder of the woman on the other side of his empty chair.

"And do you know Donna Doyle?" he said.

"Oh," said Maggie, "the romance writer?"

Donna Doyle smiled languidly and lifted her arm.

"The very one," she said.

"I see your books out all the time," said Maggie. "You're doing very well. I'm glad to know you."

"Hi," said Jackson. He didn't bother stepping up to touch the flaccid fingers. Looking across the table, he smiled. "Who are these sorry-looking characters over there?"

"Hey, Jack," said one of the three men facing him, "stop clowning around and introduce us to your wife."

"Well, this is Maggie," said Jack. Then, gesturing across the table, he went on, "Babe, these are some of the guys I know from the western writers' conference. This is Will McCarty. John Garretson, and, uh, Vaughan Hacker."

"That's not to be mistaken for hack writer," said Hacker, a bit drunkenly.

"Oh," said Maggie, "I'm sure it's not. I'm happy to meet all of you."

"Hey," said Brock. "What are you two kids drinking? I'll get it for you."

"I wouldn't mind a little glass of white wine," said Maggie.

"Coffee, Tom," said Jackson. "Black coffee."

"You sure you don't want a drink? It's all on me. Hell. The whole damn schmear."

"Thanks, Tom. Just the coffee. Okay?"

"Okay, buddy. Whatever you say," said Brock. Then he glanced at Maggie. "White wine?"

"Yes, please," she said.

Brock headed for the bar, and Maggie took Jack by the arm, pulling him toward one of the other two occupied tables in the room. As she did so, she nodded to the people at Brock's table.

"Excuse me, please," she said. "We want to say

hello over here. It was nice meeting you all. Come on, Jack."

"Yeah," said Jack. "Okay. Where are we going?"

"I want to introduce you to these people."

"See you guys," said Jack. Then he turned again to Maggie.

"Who are they? Mystery writers?"

"Yes. Well, they're one mystery writer."

"Oh, yeah?"

They reached the table, and the man and woman seated together there both looked up pleasantly at Maggie. The man stood.

"Hello, Maggie," he said.

"Hi, Charles. Joyce. I want to introduce my husband to you. Jack, these are friends of mine from the mystery writers' conventions. Meet Vance Prescott."

The two at the table chuckled at Jack's confusion, but after only a brief delay, the man extented his hand.

"Jack," he said, "I'm Charles Newton. This is my wife, Joyce. We write together under the name of Vance Prescott. Mysteries."

"Are all of Tom's clients here?" asked Joyce Newton.

"Well," said Jack, "I don't know, really, if we're all of them. A good bunch anyway."

"Won't you join us?" said Joyce.

"Thank you," said Jack, pulling out a chair for his wife.

Maggie sat down beside Joyce and leaned toward her to speak in a near whisper.

"I don't know those two over there," she said,

indicating a man and a woman at a third table, the last occupied table in the room. "Do you?"

"I don't really know them," said Joyce, "but we have been introduced. He's Douglas Wayne, and he writes adventure stuff, you know, soldier of fortune kind of things. And the woman is Robin Fletcher. She writes romance novels. Real racy ones. I read one of them one time."

"Is Bob Drago here?" asked Jackson.

Joyce looked around the room.

"Yes," she said. "Well, he was here just a minute ago. I don't see him now."

"I think he went to the john," said Charles. "He'll be back—if he didn't pass out in there."

A cowgirl-waitress walked up to the table.

"White wine?" she said.

"Right here," said Maggie.

The waitress put the wine in front of Maggie, then looked at Jackson.

"Coffee?"

"Yeah. That's right," he said.

"Cream or sugar?"

"No, thanks. Black is fine."

The cowgirl put down the coffee and turned to leave.

"Thanks," said Jackson. Then he turned back to Charles Newton. "Bob's pretty tanked up, is he?"

"He was here before we arrived," said Newton, "and he was already drunk then. He's been drinking steadily ever since."

"I don't see how the man stays on his feet," said Joyce.

Just then there was a loud bang at the other end of the room. Robert Drago had flung open

the door to the men's room from the inside,
sending it smashing into the wall. He stood
there in the open doorway for a moment weaving. The door swung back toward him, and it
bounced against his shoulder as he lurched forward. He took three bold steps, then stopped to
regain his balance. He was looking at the floor.

"Oh, God. I think he's headed this way," said
Joyce.

"Pray he doesn't make it," said Charles.

Jackson turned in his chair to look at Drago.
He felt embarrassed for his old friend, and he
was disappointed. He had been especially looking forward to renewing his acquaintance with
Drago, and he was sorry to meet him after all
these years in his present shabby state. He
pushed his chair back from the table, got up and
walked toward Drago.

"Oh, dear," said Joyce. "Are they friends?"

"We used to be very close friends with Bob
and his wife before they got a divorce. We
haven't seen him for seven years. He didn't used
to be like this."

"I'm sorry if we said anything . . ."

"No. No. It's all right," said Maggie.

Jackson walked right up to Robert Drago, who
was still looking at the floor to help him main-
tain his balance. Drago saw that someone
blocked his path. He lifted one arm as if to push
the obstacle out of his way.

"Hey," he said. "Let me through."

His voice was slurred, and he reeked of whiskey. He shirttail was pulled out of his trousers
and hanging down below his jacket. Jackson put
his hands on Drago's shoulders.

"Bob," he said. "Bob, old buddy. It's Jack Wilder. Hey. Hey, buddy."

"Jack?"

Drago worked at lifting his eyes to look into Jack's face. His eyes were small and beady and red. They looked, Jack thought, as if someone had poked a finger into each of them.

"Jack," said Drago, saliva dribbling out of one corner of his mouth. "Jack. God damn. How the hell are you? Jack. Jack."

Drago tried to put his arms around Jackson, but he couldn't quite manage the gesture. Jack was just as glad.

"Come on, Bob," he said. "Let's go sit down."

"Jack. God damn. I didn't know you were here, Jack. I love you. I love you."

"Yeah. Hell, I know that. Come on now. Come on over here and sit down. Come on."

Jackson managed to get Drago over to the table where Maggie waited with the Newtons and dropped him into a chair.

"Bob," he said. "Bob, here's Maggie. You want to say hello to Maggie?"

"Hello, Bob," said Maggie. "I'm so glad to see you again. Are you all right?"

"Yeah," slurred Drago. "I'm all right. Damn, Maggie, you look . . . Just a bit drunk is all. How long has it been? Huh? How long? I love you two. You know that? I love you both."

Charles Newton stood up and took his wife by the arm. She looked up at him, caught his meaning, and stood up from her chair.

"I think it's about time we called it quits," said Newton. "We need to change for supper. It was a pleasure meeting you."

"Maybe we'll see you at the barbecue," said Joyce.

Maggie jumped up and followed the Newtons a few steps away from the table.

"We'll catch you later," Jackson called after them.

Maggie talked in a low voice, a hand on each of the Newtons' arms.

"I'm so sorry," she said. "I know that Jack didn't mean to spoil your evening by bringing Bob over to your table."

"It's all right, Mrs. Wilder," said Newton. "We needed to leave anyway."

"Hey, you," called Bob Drago from his chair. "Fig Newtons. You don't have to leave because of me. Hell. I'll go off somewhere. Leave because of me."

"Good night, Mr. Drago," said Newton, taking his wife again by the arm and heading for the door. "I hope you feel better in the morning."

"Go on," Drago shouted after them. "Go on. Hell. I don't need you. Get the hell out of here anyway. God damn it."

The Newtons left the bar and Drago sagged back in his chair as Maggie returned to the table and sat back down.

"Say," said Drago, "what the hell did that sly bastard mean by that remark?"

"What, Bob?" said Jackson. "What remark?"

"Hope I feel better in the morning. What the hell kind of a thing to say is that?"

"Bob," said Jackson, "cut it out. Hey, buddy, cut it out. They haven't done anything to you. They're not leaving because of you. Take it easy, Bob."

"Ah, they piss me off," said Drago.

"Bob, you ought to go to bed. Don't you think you've had about enough? Huh? Come on. I'll help you."

"God damn it, Jack. Don't you start on me. Not you."

"I'm not starting on you, Bob. I just thought you might want some help getting out to your cabin. It's all right. It's all right. Hell, have another drink if you want. It's all the same to me."

Jackson was embarrassed by Drago's idiotic behavior, but he was also concerned about the well-being of a man he had once considered his best friend. He thought that he should really get Maggie away so that she wouldn't have to put up with all this. He noticed, not surprised, that everyone in the room was watching Drago with obvious disgust, but, happily, Drago fell into a sudden moody silence. Jackson took a sip of his coffee.

"Coffee's cold," he said.

Suddenly Drago lurched up from his chair.

"I need a drink," he said, and he stalked to the bar.

"My God, Jack," said Maggie, "what's happened to him?"

"I don't know, babe. I've never seen him like this before. Never. He's really soused."

"Do you suppose it's because of him and Sylvia splitting up? They were so good together. I just hated it when they got their divorce. Maybe that's what's the matter with Bob."

"Well, I just don't know."

Drago had gotten himself another drink at the bar and staggered over to the table where Brock

sat with the five others. Drago stood weaving behind Will McCarty.

"You all right?" asked Brock.

"Is this your new fair-haired boy here?" said
Drago.

"What?" said Brock.

"This right here," said Drago, pouring some of
his drink over McCarty's head.

"Hey! God damn it!" McCarty shouted and
jumped up from his chair. His sudden movement knocked Drago off balance, sending him
stumbling backwards and causing him to fall
into a chair that fortunately was unoccupied before Drago's sudden mishap.

"God damn!" said McCarty.

Jackson was across the room in a hurry, getting himself in between McCarty and Drago.

"He's drunk, man," said Jackson. "Let it go,
huh? He's so damn drunk he doesn't know what
he's doing."

"I ought to kill the bastard," said McCarty.

"Hey, it's not worth it," said Jack, holding Mc-
Carty. "You don't need to beat up a drunk. Let it
go."

Brock stood up.

"It's time we all headed out back for the barbecue," he said. "Come on, Will. Let's get it
started."

"Get it started, hell," said McCarty. "I've got to
go wash and change my shirt. God damn!"

Will McCarty pulled himself away from Jackson, gave Drago a hard look and followed Brock
out of the Old Corral. Jackson stood looking
down at Drago, who waved an arm at him in
disgust.

"Go on," he said. "Go on with them."

Jackson went to Maggie, and they followed the others out. Drago sat alone in the lounge.

"Hey," he called out. "Hey."

The cowgirl behind the bar looked around the room. There was no one else in sight.

"Yes sir?" she said.

"My drink spilled," said Drago. "Bring me another goddamn whiskey and water."

"Sir, are you sure . . . ?"

"Just bring me the goddamn drink."

The barbecue smelled delicious, and the fresh air was welcome after the smoke-filled barroom. Tom Brock had gone through at the head of the line and was just sitting down at one of the picnic tables behind the lodge when Jackson walked with Maggie to the food line.

"You go on through the line, babe," he said. "I'm going to talk to Tom a bit while I can catch him alone."

"But you . . ."

"Go on," said Jack, giving Maggie a gentle shove forward. "Go on. I'll join you in just a little bit. Okay? Go on ahead and eat."

He sauntered over to the table where Brock still sat alone and sat down beside him.

"Get yourself a plate, Jack," said Brock.

"Yeah. In a minute, Tom. Say, I want to ask you something."

"What?"

Brock wasn't wasting any words. His mouth was full of beef and bread. A little sauce ran down his chin, and he daubed at it with a paper napkin.

"Tom, what's happened to Bob? He's not the same man I knew seven years ago."

"Too much booze, Jack. He can't handle it. That's all."

"Is it because of the divorce, do you think?"

"Nope. Oh, it got worse after the divorce, but I don't think that it started then. Matter of fact, I think that it was Bob's drinking that caused the divorce."

"Damn," said Jack.

"Jack," said Brock, "put it out of your mind. There's not a damn thing you can do. Sylvia tried and gave it up. I tried. He's too far gone. He hasn't written a thing for three years now. He's living off the royalties from what he wrote years ago. Barely making it, too. I should have dumped him a long time ago. I'm just hanging on for old time's sake, I guess."

"And you're advising me to dump him?" said Jackson.

"Go get a plate," said Brock.

"Yeah. Okay."

Jack headed for the food line. Halfway over, he met Will McCarty. Taking note of the hard look McCarty was giving him, Jack was glad that McCarty's hands were filled with plates of food. The food looked good, and suddenly Jack was hungry.

"Excuse me," he said.

McCarty blocked Jack's path to the food line. He stood stock still and looked Jack in the eye.

"Don't ever step between me and that drunken sot again," he said.

Jack stepped back and held up his hands in a gesture of surrender.

"Hey," he said. "Don't worry about that. I'm not his keeper. Never happen again. No hard feelings, huh?"

McCarty didn't answer, and Jack took his place at the end of the food line. Maggie was coming out the other end and looking for a place to sit down.

Well, hell, thought Jack, *we're getting off to one hell of a start.*

Robert Drago managed to get himself out the front door of the lodge. He stood swaying on the front steps for a few seconds, taking in deep breaths of the fresh Wyoming night air, hoping that it would help to sober him up. It was no use. He had drunk too much. Much too much. He leaned back against the wall to steady himself, and he thought about better times. He thought about the times when he was writing, when his books were selling. He thought about good evenings spent with his wife, Sylvia, and their friends, Jack and Maggie Wilder. Those good times back in Oklahoma. He felt a tear well up in his right eye, and he cursed himself. Those times were over.

"To hell with them," he said.

He stepped forward and nearly fell down the steps. He managed to stay on his feet, straightened himself up and headed for a nearby jeep. He fumbled in his pocket for a key, dropped it in the dirt and then couldn't find it again. He wasn't even sure it was the right key. Come to think of it, he wasn't sure that he had approached the right jeep.

"Goddamn things are all the same," he muttered.

He turned and surveyed the grounds, laid eyes on what he was reasonably sure was the cabin to which he had been assigned, and aimed himself for it.

"To hell with them."

Drago staggered toward the cabin he hoped was his, but he caught himself veering off to the left. He stopped and stood still for a moment.

"Barbecue," he said.

He reoriented himself and started his trek again, taking more care than before. He felt good, he decided. He didn't need any of them. Jack and Maggie made him sick. *Love*, he thought with disgust. He didn't need Brock, either. Brock was sucking up to that young snot, McCarthy, Charlie McCarthy, or whatever his name was. He had read one of McCarthy's books. *Western, hell*, he thought. *What's a damn New Yorker know about the West? He wouldn't know which end of the horse to feed.*

"I'll show them all," he said. "I've got money. I've got lots of money. I don't need Brock or Wilder or Sylvia. Sylvia. Bitch."

Drago found himself at the cabin, and again he fumbled for a key. This time he managed to find one and hang on to it. He jabbed it at the door lock several times, found the hole finally, and opened the door. Leaving the key in the lock, he stumbled into the cabin. He reached weakly behind himself to shut the door, but he didn't quite make it. The door stood open. He did manage to find the light switch and turn the light on as he moved on inside the room.

"Sylvia's a bitch," he said. "I don't care. I don't care."

He staggered into the bathroom and unzipped the fly of his trousers.

"Got to take a leak."

A moment later he flushed the toilet, put both hands on the top of the tank and leaned his head against the wall. The room was spinning. No, he thought, the room couldn't be spinning. His perception was that the room was spinning. But it wouldn't stop. He thought for a few seconds that he was going to puke. He took a few deep breaths and the feeling had passed. He walked out of the bathroom and headed for the bed, but he walked past the bed to the back wall of the cabin. He turned to lean against the wall, and he noticed that the door was still standing open. *Ought to close the door*, he thought. He saw, too, that he had left the curtain drawn on the big picture window just beside the door.

"Ought to," he said. "Go to bed."

"Oh, I couldn't eat another bite," said Maggie. "It's been so long since I've had good barbecue like that."

"It's our own beef," said Dack Hunter. "Glad you liked it."

"It was a real fine meal," said Jackson. "I hope you don't have anything planned for us too early in the morning, Brock."

"Hell," said Brock, "I plan to sleep until noon."

"I thought we were going to get up early and go horseback riding," said Myrna Keck, her voice betraying disappointment.

"You get up when you want to, sweetheart," said Brock. "One of these cowboys'll be happy to ride with you."

"I don't know," said Myrna with a little whine.

Dack Hunter leaned toward her. He tipped the Stetson back on his head a little and smiled.

"You come on down here to the lodge whenever you're ready, little lady," he said. "I'll saddle up a horse for you myself and ride out with you."

"Thank you," she said, giving Brock a sly look. "Maybe I will."

"Hell, that's service," said Brock. "The boss, himself."

Hunter straightened up and looked over the crowd.

"There's more beer in the cooler, folks," he said. "Help yourselves. Or if you want something a little stronger, the bar's still open inside."

"Well," said Jackson, standing up and stretching, "I don't know about the rest of you, but I'm ready to turn in. Hell, I had breakfast this morning in Oklahoma. Been a long day."

He put a hand on Maggie's back.

"You ready?"

"Yes," she said, "I think I am. It's so nice to see all of you. Tom, this is just lovely. It was awfully good of you to invite us."

"We'll see you guys in the morning," said Jackson.

"Good night, everyone," said Maggie.

Jack and Maggie walked around the lodge to the front where they had parked the jeep. Jack pulled the key out of his pocket.

"You want to drive me home?" he said.

"Oh, no," said Maggie. "You're the one who doesn't drink. I've had a little wine and I'm just a bit woozy."

"All right," said Jack. He put an arm around Maggie's shoulders and held her close to him as he walked her to the passenger's side of the jeep. He helped her into the seat, then went around to the other side to climb in behind the wheel. He drove the short distance to the cabin, noticing on the way that the curtains were drawn, the door standing open and the lights on in the cabin of Bob Drago. There was no jeep parked there either. He parked his jeep in front of his and Maggie's cabin and helped Maggie out, holding her close again.

"I like it when you're close to me," he said.

Maggie giggled.

"Do you?" she said.

"Yes, I sure do. Believe me. I do."

Jack unlocked the door and they went inside. Without turning on the light, he shut and locked the door, then he turned Maggie around and pressed her back to the door.

"Are you going to turn on the light?" she asked.

"No."

He kissed her.

"Turn on the light, Jack."

"No," he said. "I don't want to."

He kissed her again, longer than before. She put her arms around him.

"Jack," she said quietly in his ear.

"Yeah?"

"Turn on the light so we can get ready for bed."

"Oh," he said. "Yeah. That sounds like a good idea."

It was a ludicrous paradox. The bow and arrow is among the most ancient and primitive of weapons. This one, though, was a shining testament to modern technology: all metal and fiberglass, a thin steel cable instead of a string, pulleys, weights and counterweights, even a telescopic sight. The hands that held this sleek and awesome instrument of destruction and nocked the hunting arrow with its four lethal steel blades were gloved in thin black leather. It took a strong and steady pull to bring the cable to the balance point—the point at which the tension suddenly is released and the archer's right hand glides with ease back to his eye. He stood there for an instant, seemingly frozen in time, the bow held by pressure alone against his open left hand, the drunken man in the cabin clearly visible in the sight through the open door.

The fool, he thought. *He's making it so easy.*

The door was open, the curtain on the big picture window drawn, and the lights were on. He inhaled deeply, steadied his aim, and began to expel his breath slowly as he relaxed his two crooked fingers to allow the steel cable to slip free, sending the deadly missile hurtling with incredible velocity through the open cabin door.

A brief moment of satisfaction, of exhilaration, was followed by thoughts of urgent expediency. The figure of the archer moved quickly to the jeep that was parked, not in front of the cabin, but off to one side of the lodge. He tossed the compound bow and the extra arrow onto the floor behind the jeep's front seats, found the keys in the dirt there beside the vehicle, where he had seen the man drop them, and stuck them in the ignition. Then he ran into the shadows behind the lodge and vanished.

Chapter Three

"I WONDER WHAT Brock and Hunter have cooked up for us this morning?" said Maggie, as she ran a brush quickly through her hair.

Jackson pulled on his second boot and worked the leg of his jeans down over the boot top. He reached for his denim vest.

"No telling," he said, "but I hope they've got a big breakfast for starts. You about ready?"

"My hair just looks awful, but I don't guess there's much I can do about that, so I guess I'm ready."

Jackson went to the door and opened it.

"A beautiful morning," he said.

"Wait a minute," said Maggie. "I don't know about these shoes. I'd better wear a different pair of shoes."

"Well, change your shoes then," said Jack,

standing in the doorway and looking out at the Wyoming expanse beyond the lodge.

"Now don't get impatient with me. I'll just be a minute."

"Take your time," said Jackson. "Take your time."

"All right. I'm ready now."

"Three or four jeeps already down at the lodge," said Jackson. "I hope they left us something to eat."

Maggie was at the door.

"Oh, wait a minute," she said. "Where's my purse?"

"Right over there on the chair, sweet thing. Grab it and let's go. I'm about to starve to death."

"I don't believe that you're about to starve to death," said Maggie as she ran across the room for her purse. "I don't believe that for a minute."

She stopped beside the bed, dropped her purse on the bedside table and straightened up a pillow.

"Jack," she said, "get ahold of the other side of this sheet here. Help me straighten up the bed."

"What do we need to straighten up the bed for? We're not going to have any company in here. I don't think anyone's going to come calling."

"Come on. Help me."

Jackson grabbed the sheet and helped Maggie to pull it tight. Then she took hold of the blanket.

"Get that side," she said.

"We're just going to mess it up again tonight," said Jack as he helped to smooth the top blanket. "Can we go now?"

"Yes, we can," said Maggie, grabbing up her purse. She was out the door in a flash. "Are you coming?"

Jack walked out and shut the door behind him, then turned to walk toward the lodge.

"Did you lock the door?" said Maggie.

"Naw," he said. "I don't think so."

He tested the door and found it unlocked.

"Nope," he said. "Do you want it locked?"

"Well, I think we'd better lock it. Don't you?"

"If it will make you feel better, I'll lock it," said Jack, and he reached around for the inside button on the doorknob that locked the door. "There. It's locked."

He shut the door and Maggie looked panic-stricken.

"Oh," she said, "do you have the key?"

Jackson reached down into a pocket of his jeans and pulled out a key, which he dangled in front of her.

"Yeah," he said. "Got it right here."

"Oh, good. Let's go to the lodge now and see if we can get us something to eat."

"That's a good idea," said Jack. "Why didn't I think of that?"

"Are we going to take the jeep?"

"No, let's just walk over, huh? It's a short walk. Come on."

They did make it to breakfast. They were not the first there, but neither were they the last. Then breakfast was served in a buffet line with plenty of everything, and Jackson ate voraciously. He noticed that Robert Drago was conspicuous by his absence, and he wanted to ask if anyone had seen anything of him, but he couldn't quite bring himself to do it. When just about everyone had finished eating, Dack Hunter stood up at the end of one table and tapped his coffee cup with a spoon to get attention.

"Folks," he called out, "let me have your attention here for just a minute."

The murmurs died down and Hunter continued.

"We've got a little excursion planned for you this morning. Monte Clark—most of you've met Monte, I think—Monte's outside right now saddling up enough horses for all of you, and we've got a fully outfitted chuckwagon all hitched up and ready to go. The chuckwagon is being driven by a real cowboy cook—we call him Sourdough—and we're all going to take a ride on horseback up into the mountains a ways. The chuckwagon will follow along, and by the time we get where we're going, it'll be lunchtime. We'll stop and we'll have a regular working cowboy's meal prepared for us by Sourdough right out on the open range of Wyoming. Now, you don't have to go, of course, and for anyone who decides to stay behind, a cook will be here in the lodge, but I hope all of you will ride along. I know you'll enjoy it, and if you miss it, well, you'll have missed the real Wyoming ranch experience. The horses are all gentle and easy to handle, and Monte and I will both be along to give you any help you might need. Let me tell you, folks, there's nothing tastes as good as a real good meal out on the range. It's a beautiful day out there—not too hot—so let's all gather up out at the chuckwagon."

"Oh, Jack," said Maggie, "let's go. Are we going on this thing?"

"I don't know about you, but I wouldn't miss it for anything," said Jack. "Let's go out there and look at the horses."

Outside the horses were gathered and saddled and the wagon was ready to roll. Sourdough sat impatiently on the wagon seat, reins in hand, scowling. Monte Clark smiled when he saw Jack and Maggie approaching.

"Good morning, folks," he said. "I was hoping that you'd be coming along on this little trail ride. Miz Wilder, I brought those books for you to sign for me. Do you mind?"

"Oh, no," said Maggie. "I don't mind. Where are they?"

Clark reached in the saddlebags on his horse and pulled out three hardcover copies of Maggie Wilder mysteries. He took a pen out of his shirt pocket and handed it to her.

"How are you going to go about passing out these horses?" said Jack, his eye on a big Appaloosa.

"You're the first ones out here," said Clark. "Take your pick."

Maggie was writing in Clark's books against the saddle of his horse. She finished the third inscription and handed the book and pen to Clark, who immediately opened the covers to see what she had written.

"Thank you, Monte," she said.

"Oh, thank you, Miz Wilder. Say, that's real nice," said Monte, tucking the books carefully back into the saddlebags. "Now you just pick out the horse you want. Whichever one you want."

"Oh, I don't know," said Maggie. "I really don't know how to make up my mind. They're all so pretty."

"Then let me pick one for you," said Clark. "It'd be my pleasure. May I?"

"Yes, please," she said.

Monte Clark led Maggie to the side of a pinto mare and handed her the reins.

"She's just about my favorite," he said. "She's a good horse."

Maggie climbed into the saddle.

"Thank you, Monte," she said. "She is nice."

Tom Brock and Will McCarty walked up just then, and Jackson looked back toward the lodge to see the others coming outside.

"Tom," he said, "I think I'll take a quick run over to the cabins to check on Bob. You haven't seen him, have you?"

"You'll just find him passed out," said Brock, "but go ahead if it will make you feel any better."

Jackson climbed into the saddle of the big Appaloosa and turned it toward the cabin with the open door.

"I'll be right back, Maggie," he said.

He trotted the horse over to the cabin and stopped in front of the door. Sitting in the saddle he called out.

"Bob. Hey, Bob."

There was no answer. He shouted louder.

"Hey, Bob Drago. You in there?"

Tom Brock came riding up and stopped beside Jackson. There was still no answer from inside the cabin.

"Tom," said Jackson, "the door's still open from last night. That's the way he left it last night. Door open. Curtain pulled back and the lights on."

"It's like I told you," said Brock. "He went in there and passed out. He probably won't come out of it until sometime this afternoon. Come on. Forget it."

"Well," said Jackson, leaning over and squinting into the room, "you're probably right. He was pretty damn drunk, I know. Just a minute."

Jackson swung down out of the saddle and walked to the open door. He put a hand on the doorjamb and leaned into the cabin. Looking around, he saw no sign of Robert Drago. The bathroom door was open, too. No one in there. Then something on the far wall caught his eye.

"Hey. What the hell's that?" he said.

"What?" said Brock.

"Tom, come here."

"What the hell is it?" said Brock, getting off his horse.

As Brock approached the door, Jackson stepped into the room.

"He's not here," said Jackson. "He's not in here, but look at that."

On the far wall a hunting arrow was buried a good six inches into the wood and plaster about chest high to a man. The room was a mess, and Robert Drago was nowhere in sight.

* * *

The whole gang soon had gathered around the mystery cabin, and they had abandoned their mounts and started to crowd inside to see what all the fuss was about. Maggie pushed her way through the crowd and into the room to find Jackson.

"Jack," she said. "Jack, what's wrong? What's going on here?"

"Maggie, something's happened to Bob. He's not here. No one's seen him today. The cabin's just like he left it last night, and, uh, then there's that thing."

He pointed to the sinister black shaft in the wall.

"Oh, my God," she said. "Do you think something's happened to him, really?"

"Yes, I do."

"Well, then don't you think we'd better get all these people out of here?"

"Huh?"

"There might be some clues around here or something. Or there might have been before everyone started tramping around in here."

"Damn," said Jack, "you're right. Hey, hey. Everybody out. Outside. Come on folks, clear out of here, will you? Brock, help me get all of these people out of here."

"Move out, friends," said Brock in a loud and commanding voice. "Let's all get back over to the chuckwagon. We need to get started. Let's go."

With only a little difficulty, Brock managed to get them all back to the wagon with Hunter and Clark and Sourdough, who had not moved from his wagon seat, and ready to start the ride. Jack, Maggie and Brock remained behind in the cabin.

"Tom," said Jackson, "we can't go off on a damned excursion. Not now. We've got to find out what's happened to Bob."

"What makes you think that anything's happened to him?" said Brock.

"Well, where is he?"

"Who knows? Who knows where a drunk goes or what he does or why?"

"The place is wide open. The lights on."

"Just like he left them last night," said Brock. "You said it, yourself. He was too drunk to care."

"But what about that arrow?" said Maggie.

"Hell," said Brock, "I don't know. Drago probably shot it into the wall for some drunken reason. I don't know what you're so damned worried about. Look, you two don't know him like I do. Not anymore. He's crazy, and I'm not going to let him spoil this celebration. Now are you coming or not?"

"No, Tom," said Jackson. "No. I think we ought to call the sheriff."

Brock walked to the open door and waved wildly in the direction of the waiting riders.

"Monte," he called out. "Monte. Come over here a minute, will you?"

Monte Clark spurred his pony and galloped over to the cabin.

"Yes sir?"

"Monte," said Brock, "the brochure the ranch sent out mentions the hunting up here, doesn't it?"

"That's right."

"Does it say anything about bow hunting?"

"Yes sir, I believe it does."

"Do you remember if anyone brought a bow along with them? Was there a bow in the luggage that you can recall?"

"Yeah," said Monte, shoving his hat back and scratching his head. "I seem to remember one of them fancy things—what do you call them? You know, real modern thing."

"A compound bow?" said Jack.

"Yeah," said Clark. "That's what they call them. Compound bow. There was one of them."

Jack walked over to the shaft in the wall and gave it a tug. It didn't budge.

"That makes sense," he said. "It would take a compound bow to drive an arrow into the wall like this."

"Whose bow was it?" asked Maggie. "Do you remember who brought it?"

"No," said Clark. "It was the day I picked up a whole van full of folks. Back of the van was full of bags and stuff. I don't remember who brought the bow."

"Could it have been Drago?" asked Brock.

"Drago was in that bunch. Yes sir. It could have been his. I really don't know. Sorry. Is there anything else? We ought to be getting started."

"No, that's all, Monte," said Brock, then added quickly, "Wait a minute. Where's the jeep assigned to Drago?"

"Why, uh, it was over at the lodge last night," said Clark. He stretched himself in the saddle and looked around. "I don't see it anywhere this morning."

"Thanks, Monte," said Brock.

Monte Clark tipped his hat and turned his horse to ride back to the chuckwagon. Brock turned impatiently on Jackson.

"Okay?" he said. "The jeep's gone. Bob had the keys. He staggered in here drunk last night, turned the lights on, and then for some reason or other, he took the jeep and went off someplace. Probably to look for another drink."

"What about the arrow?" said Jack.

"He shot that into the wall before he left."

"Then where's the bow?" asked Maggie.

"It's probably in the jeep with Bob. Listen, you two, I've had it. You're two of my favorite people, but I'm not going to let even you spoil this week. I'm going on this ride, and I wish you'd come along with me. Whatever you do, I'm going."

"I'm going to call the sheriff, Tom," said Jack.

"Do what you want," said Brock as he mounted his horse to ride back to join the others. "If you decide that you're wasting your time, see if you can catch up with us."

"Why don't you go on ahead with the others, Maggie?" said Jack. "Hell, Tom might be right. Probably is. I'll see what the sheriff has to say, and then I'll try to catch up."

"Oh, I don't know," said Maggie. "Are you sure?"

"Yeah, sure. You go on ahead. I'll catch up."

"Well, all right. I will. You try not to let this worry you too much. Okay? See what the sheriff has to say. Promise?"

"Yeah," said Jack. "Don't worry. I'll be okay."

"I love you, Jack," said Maggie, and she kissed

him, then mounted the pinto and rode to join the crowd.

Jackson Wilder stood for a long moment in the room alone. He thought that the room should have something to tell him, but it didn't. There was only the general mess, the steel shaft in the wall, the lights still burning, the drawn curtain and the open door with the key in the lock. He left the cabin and headed for the lodge to find a phone.

Maggie rode alongside Monte Clark at the head of the group of riders. Will McCarty jounced along trying to ride English style sitting in a western saddle. The chuckwagon brought up the rear. The trail had led away from the lodge and up into the rising mountains. The air was clean, clear and crisp, and Maggie drew it into her lungs in great gulps.

"Oh, Monte," she said, "it's beautiful up here."

"Yes, ma'am, it sure is. I like it. I wouldn't live anywhere else in the world. Especially not in a city, I wouldn't."

"Monte."

"Yes?"

"Monte, are those jeep tracks?"

Maggie pointed to a set of tire tracks which headed straight up the mountain trail. In fact, the riders might have been following the tracks.

"Yeah," said Monte. "Them's jeep tracks, all right."

"Can you tell how old they are?"

"Well," said the young cowboy, "I ain't no expert tracker, but I'd say they were fairly recent."

"Like maybe sometime last night?"

"Maybe."

"Monte, is there any reason for anyone to have been up here recently in a jeep?"

"Well, I can't think of one, Miz Wilder," said Clark. "I can't think of any. I think all the jeeps are assigned to you folks right now. Except for the one I drive. Mr. Hunter drives his Cadillac, mostly. Nope. I can't figure who made those tracks."

Bob Drago, Maggie thought, *or someone in Bob's jeep*, but she kept the thought to herself. For the time being, they were following the tracks anyway. She would wait a while and see how things developed. Maggie looked back over her shoulder. She wished that Jack would hurry and catch up with them. She wondered how things had gone with the sheriff.

"How much farther, Monte?" she asked.

"Oh, we've got a ways to go yet," answered the cowboy. "We'll stop up here around the bend and take a short rest. There's a spot up there with a real great view. You can look down on the whole valley. It's one of my favorite spots on the whole ranch. I sometimes ride up here by myself and just set and look."

"It sounds real nice."

They rode ahead, Maggie with anticipation, both for the rest and the view that would accompany it and in hopes of discovering something up ahead by means of the jeep tracks. Tom Brock urged his horse forward, somewhat clumsily, and caught up with Maggie. Then he slowed down again to ride beside her. Monte Clark politely allowed some space to develop between his mount and Maggie's on her other side.

"Is this great?" said Brock.

"Great, Tom. This was really a marvelous idea you had. I wish Jack would hurry up and join us."

"He's just got to come to grips with the fact that his old buddy has become a hopeless alcoholic," said Brock.

"Is anyone ever really hopeless, Tom?"

"Well, I don't know, but if anyone ever was, it's Bob Drago."

"They were such good friends," said Maggie.

"I know they were," said Brock. "I know it's tough on Jack, and I'm sorry to be impatient with him, but I've been putting up with Drago all this time. You two haven't seen him for—how long now?"

"It's been about seven years," said Maggie. "Until last night."

"Well, Jack'll get over it."

They rounded the bend and a vast and beautiful panorama opened up before them. Maggie drew in a deep breath. The view was stunning. Monte hadn't exaggerated a bit, she thought.

"Oh, look," she said.

"Here we are, folks," called out Monte Clark.

There was a wide level spot off the side of the road, protected from the sharp drop off by a rail fence. Monte had the riders dismount and tether the horses to the rail. The chuckwagon pulled up, and Sourdough set the brake.

"Cold drinks over here," he called out as he climbed down from the wagon seat.

Maggie started to join the others in their rush for the chuckwagon, but she decided, as she would obviously have to wait in line anyway, to take in the view just a bit longer first. She thought that she could understand why this was Monte Clark's favorite spot. She looked out over the vast expanse, almost becoming dizzy with its grandeur. Then she allowed her eyes to follow the rail fence on up the road. Suddenly she turned and ran back for the pinto.

"Monte," she called out as she climbed into the saddle.

"What is it?" Clark answered, but Maggie was already riding on ahead. Clark jumped on his horse and followed her. She stopped not far ahead, and as Clark rode up to join her, he saw what had attracted her attention. The jeep tracks veered off the road and the fence rails were smashed where the tracks went through. Clark and Maggie exchanged a glance. Then they dismounted.

"Careful," said Clark. He took Maggie's hand as they stepped over the broken rails to get closer to the edge.

"There it is," she said.

Far below they could see the overturned jeep.

"Oh, no," said Maggie. "Poor Bob."

"We don't know that he's down there, Miz Wilder," said Clark. "Let's go back to the others. I'll tell Mr. Hunter and Mr. Brock what we found. We can't get down there from here anyway. We'll have to ride on ahead another mile or so. Either that or all the way back down to the lodge and start over from that direction."

They got back on their horses and rode down to where the others were gathered around the chuckwagon. Monte drew Hunter and Brock aside, just as Maggie saw Jackson riding alone up the trail. She jerked the reins of the pinto and rode to meet him.

"Jack," she said, "I'm so glad you made it. The jeep is off the road up there ahead."

"Well, let's go," he said.

"No. Wait. Monte says we can't get down to it from here. We have to ride on ahead some. He's telling Tom and Mr. Hunter about it right now."

"Come on."

They rode on up to where Monte Clark was filling Brock and Hunter in on the details. The three men looked up at Jack with concern on their faces.

"Hey," Jack said, "we've got to get on up there and check that jeep out."

"We're trying to figure out how best to handle this, Wilder," said Hunter.

"Hell, you can stop figuring. Bob might be hurt down there. You going to show me the way, or do I have to look for it by myself?"

Hunter turned to Clark.

"Take him down there, Monte," he said. "I'll stay here with the excursion. There's no need to alarm anyone else."

"Okay, let's go," said Jack.

Monte Clark ran for his horse. As he rode past Hunter and Brock to join Jackson, Hunter called out to him.

"You find anything down there," he said, "come back and let us know. In the meanwhile we'll just continue on our way like there was nothing wrong. You got that?"

"Yes, sir," said Clark.

* * *

Monte Clark and Jackson Wilder were soon at the spot where the jeep had gone over the edge. They stopped and Clark showed the jeep to Jack. Jack took a quick look, then ran back to the Appaloosa.

"Come on," he said.

They rode on a mile or so before Monte Clark turned his mount toward the edge.

"This way," he said. "It's steep. Be careful."

"I'm all right," said Jackson. "You just lead the way."

Clark was right. They could get down at this place, but it wasn't easy. The Appaloosa hunkered his hindquarters down close to the ground to skitter down the sharp incline. Jackson leaned back in the saddle. There was only one way to go, so Jackson didn't have to worry about the Appaloosa following the lead of Clark and his mount. It was a frightening ride, but there was no way Jackson would have let Clark know that. He was determined to show the snot-nosed young cowboy that he could handle a horse just as well as the next man. When it came to horsemanship, Wyoming had nothing over Oklahoma, by God. They finally reached a more or less level place. It was a kind of ledge that would lead them over to where the jeep lay overturned. Jackson pulled the bandanna out of his rear pocket to wipe the sweat and the dust from his face.

"It's an easy ride from here," said Clark.

"Glad to hear it," said Jackson.

When they arrived at the jeep, Jackson quickly dismounted and ran to the overturned vehicle.

He squatted down and looked underneath. He stood up and looked around. There was no sign of a body. No footprints led away from the wreck.

"Is this Drago's jeep?" he asked Clark.

"Yeah," said Clark. "It is."

"But no sign of Drago," said Jackson.

"I sure don't see none," said Clark.

Jackson squatted down once more to look under the jeep. This time he took more care. He was no longer anticipating the possibility of discovering a body. He didn't know what he was looking for. Maggie would have said, "clues."

"Hey."

"What you got?" said Clark.

Jackson stood up and gestured toward the jeep.

"Underneath there," he said. "Compound bow."

"You have to admit that it's all very strange," said Maggie.

"Maggie," said Brock, "everything about Bob Drago for several years now has been strange."

"I think Pudge is going to feel like he's been called out on another wild goose chase," said Hunter.

Over at the bar in The Old Corral, Jackson Wilder hung up the telephone and moved to rejoin Maggie and the others at the table.

"Well, he said he'd be right out," said Jack. "Didn't sound too pleased about it, though."

"Pudge Evans is a good sheriff," said Hunter. "Hell, I headed up his last campaign. He's a good man, but he came out here once already this morning for you, Wilder. Listening to your wild stories. Found no evidence of anything wrong. Now you've called him out again. You don't expect him to be pleased with you, do you?"

"I expect the man to do his job, Hunter. Isn't that why you campaigned for him? Because he'd do his job? I don't understand you people. Something's wrong here. Bob Drago has disappeared. Someone shot an arrow into the wall of his cabin last night, his jeep has been run off the mountain, and he's disappeared, and nobody seems to give a damn. What the hell's the matter with you people?"

"Jack," said Brock, "the man is a drunk."

"Yeah," said Jackson, "and his life was threatened right in this room just last night."

"Hey, now, Jack," said Brock, "that's going a little too far. I've put up with you this far, but when you start making accusations against one of my clients, and a friend of mine, that's too much."

"You don't want to put up with me, Tom, you don't have to put up with me. Hunter, you give me the bill for me and Maggie, you hear? Brock's not paying our way. You give me the bill. You hear me?"

"Sure," said Hunter, "whatever you say. I don't give a damn one way or the other as long as I get paid."

"Yeah," said Jack, "that's about the way I had you figured."

"What the hell's that supposed to mean?" said Hunter.

Maggie put a hand on Jackson's arm.

"Jack," she said, "take it easy. Don't get all excited. The sheriff is coming out to investigate."

She turned to Brock and continued.

"Tom, Jack didn't accuse anyone of anything. He just means that there's plenty of reason for some concern. We don't know what's made Bob behave the way he's been, but he was our friend. And after all, Tom, we're your clients, too, and, I thought, your friends."

Brock stood up quickly from the table and paced away a few steps. He ran his hands over his face and through his hair.

"Dammit," he said. "You are my friends. That's why you're here. This whole thing has just got me so wrought up that I'm not thinking straight. I had such great plans for this week. It was supposed to be a celebration. It wasn't supposed to be like this. I don't mean to be fighting you, Jack."

Jackson sat quiet at the table.

"Jack?"

Still getting no answer, Brock walked back to the table. He extended his right hand in front of Jackson.

"Jack," he said, "we're friends. Let me pay the bill. All right? That was the original agreement. It's like a contract, Jack. Come on. Let me pay it. Please. Look, I'm sorry that I haven't shown enough concern for Bob. We'll investigate this thing. Okay? Are you going to let me pay your goddamned bill, you goddamn ornery old cuss?"

Jackson allowed a grin to appear on his face. He took hold of Brock's hand and looked Brock in the eye.

"Hell, yeah," he said, "you can pay the bill if

you feel that strong about it, Tom. You listening to all this, Hunter?"

Hunter raised his arms in a gesture of unconcern just as the door opened and Monte Clark stepped in.

"Mr. Hunter," he said, "Sheriff Evans is here."

Jackson rose quickly from his chair.

"Come on, Maggie," he said. They rushed out the door to meet the sheriff, Brock and Hunter following at a somewhat more leisurely pace.

"Thanks for getting back out here so quickly, Sheriff," said Jack, outside the front door of the lodge. He extended his right hand, and the big lawman gripped it hard in his meaty paw.

"It's all in the job," he said.

"This is my wife, Maggie," said Jack.

"Pleased to meet you, Sheriff Evans," said Maggie.

"Pudge, ma'am, just Pudge," said the sheriff, tipping his hat to Maggie. "So you found the jeep?"

"Yeah," said Jack. "That's right. It ran off the mountain road just a few miles up that way."

"Well, I suppose that I'll have to go check it out."

Just then Brock and Hunter came walking up, and Pudge Evans turned to the ranch owner.

"Dack," he said, "do you suppose that you could make me the loan of a horse to get over to that jeep? I understand you can't get to it no other way."

"Sure, Pudge. I'll have Monte saddle one up for you right away."

"While we're waiting," said the sheriff, "why don't you tell me just exactly what you seen?"

"There's not much to tell," said Jackson. "Maggie first saw where the tracks went off the road."

"I was watching the tracks as we were riding up the trail," said Maggie, "and I asked Monte if anyone had any reason to be driving a jeep up that road recently. He said that he didn't know of any. Then later I saw where the tracks went off the road and the rails were broken. We had to walk right up to the edge, though, before we could actually see the jeep."

"Then when I came along—that was right after I left you down here—I rode with Monte on down to take a look at the jeep. It was Bob Drago's jeep, all right, and there's a compound bow underneath it. No sign of Bob or of anyone else. That's about it."

"Well," said Pudge, "I believe you, but I'll go look for myself. Take a few pictures. I might as well tell you right now, though, that if I don't find any more than what you just described to me, we're still where we were before. There's nothing for me to do."

"But Bob's disappeared," said Maggie.

"From what I've heard, Miz Wilder, Bob Drago was liable to do just about anything last night, including to disappear. My understanding is that he had the keys to the jeep. That means that he must have drove it up there. A drunk could have easily drove off the road like that. Then you say there's a compound bow at the site. If Drago had the jeep and the bow's in the jeep, then Drago must have shot the arrow into the cabin wall."

"But if Bob drove off the mountain," said Jackson, "why didn't we find him down there?"

"Mr. Wilder," said Pudge, "I've dealt with a good many drunks in my day. It's absolutely amazing what a drunk can sometimes come through without a scratch. He could be anywhere. My advice is that if you haven't heard from him by midnight tomorrow, that'll be forty-eight hours, or at least close enough, then you come in to my office the next morning, and we'll file a missing-person report. That's all we can do. We've got no evidence of any crime, not unless I find something up there that you missed."

Monte Clark rode up on his horse leading another for the sheriff. Pudge turned to mount up.

"I'm sorry," he said, "but that's how it looks to me right now. If I see it any different later, I'll let you know."

Leather creaked as the big man climbed into the saddle. He tipped his hat to Maggie, then nudged the horse forward, following Monte Clark toward the mountain road.

Chapter Four

MAGGIE ROLLED OVER in bed. Automatically, she reached out for Jackson, and the empty space there beside her brought her out of her sleep. It was late night and dark inside the cabin, and it took a while before Maggie could see even the shapes around her.

"Jack?" she said. "Jack, where are you?"

"I'm right over here, babe."

She looked toward the sound of his voice, her eyes beginning to focus a little better, and found him standing in the open doorway.

"What's wrong, Jack?" she said.

"Ah, I just couldn't sleep. It's a beautiful night out. Clear. Come and look at the stars."

Maggie crawled out of the bed and went to Jackson's side. He put an arm around her and pulled her close to him. After thirty years of marriage, he still thrilled at the closeness of her, at her feel and at her smell.

"It is lovely," she said, looking up at the sky. "Jack, honey, are you sure you're all right?"

"You know," he said, "maybe something's wrong with me. Maybe everyone else is right about Bob. He got drunk as a skunk, shot an arrow into the wall of his cabin and drove the jeep off the road. He was so damn drunk that he didn't get hurt, just bounced on down the hillside in a grand and glorious stupor, and then he just wandered off somewhere. That's what they all think. And there's really nothing to indicate that anything else happened. Nothing except the way I remember Bob."

He paused, and Maggie hugged him close to her. She kissed his bare chest.

"And he's not the way I remember him," Jack said. "He's not at all what I remember."

"I guess these things happen to people," said Maggie.

Jack kissed Maggie on the forehead.

"Yeah," he said. "Hey. Let's go back to bed. Come on."

He crossed over to the bed and flopped himself down across it. Maggie still stood in the doorway looking out at the night.

"You coming?" said Jack.

"Jack," she said with a sudden urgency in her voice. "Jack, come here."

"What?"

"Come here. There's a light."

Jack jumped up from the bed and hurried back to her side in the doorway.

"Where?" he said. "What are you talking about?"

"Over there. At Bob's cabin. There's a light."

"By God, you're right. It looks like someone's in there with a flashlight. It's moving around a little bit. You think it's a flashlight?"

"Yes, I think so. That's what it looks like. What are we going to do?"

"You're going to stay here," said Jack.

He fumbled in the dark for his jeans.

"Well," said Maggie, "you're not going over there by yourself."

"Hey," he said, pulling on his trousers, "what were we just saying? It's probably just old Bob come back off his drunk. Okay? Don't worry. I'm just going to check it out. Take a peek."

"Why would Bob be using a flashlight?"

"Hell, I don't know," he said, "but I'm fixing to find out. Now you stay here. You hear me?"

Jack ran out the door and headed through the dark night toward the Drago cabin. He ran about halfway, then slowed to a walk, something inside telling him that he should be a little cautious. When he got close to the cabin, he began to step easy. He inched up to the door. It was still open, and the key was still in the lock. He stood quietly beside the open door for a few seconds, his heart pounding in his chest. He wondered who had turned the light off and when. A funny thing to wonder about, he thought. He took deep breaths to keep himself from panting noisily, and even then he thought that the breaths were loud. He could see the light moving inside, and he could hear, now that he stood at the open door, the sounds of rummaging. Someone was inside looking for something. The cabins were all built alike, and Jack thought that he could find the light switch just inside the door without any trouble. He could think of only one thing to do.

Taking a deep breath, he stepped quickly into the doorway and found the light switch with one fast slap to the wall. The sudden flood of light was momentarily blinding, but in an instant he could see the form of a crouched figure on the other side of the room, seemingly frozen, one hand in a dresser drawer, a flashlight in his other hand, and looking at Jack, his eyes big with fright.

"What are you doing here?" asked Jack.

The figure straightened suddenly and hurled the heavy-duty flashlight across the room at Jack's head. Jack dove to one side, the flashlight flying past his head and out through the open door.

"Hey," he shouted.

The man ran for the door, but Jack was back up and blocking the way again, so he stopped and backed up a few steps. He was in a crouch, ready to spring.

"Get out of my way," he said.

"Wait a minute," said Jack. "Just wait a minute."

The stranger looked around himself with jerky eye movements and swung his arm out to grab and toss in one motion a table lamp that he found off to his right side. The force of the toss ripped the plug out of the wall socket, but the jerked cord slowed the flight of the lamp enough for Jack to duck that one, too. The lamp smashed against the doorjamb. As Jack was dodging this latest missile, he could see the man reaching inside his coat for something. He flung himself at the man with all his strength, causing them both to fall through the bathroom door and tumble into the tub. A gun flew from the man's hand and clattered against the porcelain. The man's pudgy hands went to Jack's throat, but Jack, being on top, had the advantage. The other had fallen backwards into the tub, his knees draped over the edge. Jack took hold of the fat wrists to try to pry the hands loose from his throat. A line from *Hamlet* flashed through his mind: "I prithee, take thy fingers from my throat." Leaning over the tub the way he was, Jack was badly off balance, but holding tight to the wrists and bracing his knees against the tub, he pulled back as hard as he could, hauling the man to his feet. As the bulk came up out of the tub, Jack stumbled against the commode and fell backwards against the wall. The man released his grip and bolted out the door.

"Hey," Jack called out, "come back here."

He regained his balance and ran after the man. Outside in the dark, he stopped. He hadn't seen which way the man went. Just then Maggie ran up beside him.

"He ran toward the lodge," she said.

Jack started to run after the man, but the sound of an engine starting up stopped him. A dark station wagon backed away from the lodge.

"Damn!"

Jack ran for the jeep parked in front of his cabin, at the same time fumbling in his pocket for the keys. They weren't there. He ran into the cabin, hitting the light switch as he entered, found the keys on a table and ran back outside to vault into the jeep. Maggie came running after him.

"Jack," she called out. "Wait. What do you think you're doing?"

"Call Pudge," Jack shouted as he fumbled the key into the ignition.

As Maggie ran toward the lodge, she heard the jeep's engine roar to a start. Jack jammed the gearshift lever into reverse and popped the clutch, backing away from the cabin. He ground the gears getting into low, then flung dirt and gravel behind him as he tore off after the station wagon. It had a good head start on him, but it was headed down the long drive toward the highway, and it was blowing blue smoke out its behind. When Jack got the station wagon in the headlights of the jeep, he could see that it was a Chevrolet. An Impala, dark blue, he thought, and about a 1973 model. He pressed the gas pedal to the floor of the jeep, and the engine made a painfully high-pitched whine. Just as he thought he was getting about all there was to get out of the four-cylinder engine, the Impala made the turn onto the highway. Jack tried to slow for the turn, but he was too late. He had been too intent on trying to catch his man, and the speed at which he was traveling was too much for the balance of the jeep to take in making the turn to the highway. For a terrible instant, Jack thought that he was going to roll the jeep, but instead he shot across the road and into the ditch on the other side. He managed to turn the wheels and run the jeep straight down the ditch until it had slowed enough to drive it back up onto the highway. The Impala was long gone. Jack pulled over to the side of the road and parked.

"Damn," he said, hitting the steering wheel in his frustration. He could feel the hard and fast pounding of his heart in his chest, and he noticed that he had begun to shake uncontrollably.

"Damn!"

The whole place was astir. Everyone was awake and lights were on at the lodge and in all of the cabins. The sheriff's car drove up, and Dack Hunter walked over to it to greet Pudge Evans.

"You got an extra cabin, Dack?" asked Pudge. "I might just as well just move on out here."

"I'm sorry about all this, Pudge," said Hunter.

Jackson Wilder was walking up to the two men, and Pudge Evans hauled himself out from behind the wheel of the sheriff's car.

"Never mind, Dack," he said. "I'm just pulling your leg. It's all part of the job. Now what's this all about?"

Maggie ran up behind Jack.

"Sheriff Evans," she said. "I'm so glad you're here."

Pudge touched the brim of his hat.

"Ma'am," he said. "What happened out here?"

"There was a light on in the cabin," said Maggie.

"The cabin Drago was assigned?"

"That's right. Jack couldn't sleep, so he was up, and then I couldn't sleep either, so I got up, and we were standing in the doorway just looking at the stars, you know. Well, Jack went back to bed, and I was just about to, but then I saw the light."

"In the cabin?"

"Yes."

"I went over to investigate," said Jack. "I thought that maybe it was Bob come back, so I went on over there, and I turned on the light. Well, it wasn't Bob."

"Wait a minute," said Pudge. "You turned on the light? You said there was a light on already."

"No," said Maggie. "What we saw was a flashlight."

"The man in the cabin had a flashlight," said Jack, "and he was searching the place. Looking for something. The flashlight's over there on the ground. He threw it at me."

"Go on," said Pudge.

"Well," Jack said, "after he threw the light, he came at me. We struggled for a minute or so, I don't know, and he pulled a gun. In the scuffle, he dropped it. It's in there in the bathtub."

"In the bathtub? Go on."

"That's about it, Sheriff. He got loose from me, or maybe I got loose from him, and he ran out in the dark. I lost sight of him, but Maggie saw where he ran to. He ran toward the lodge. I guess he had his car parked over there, because the next thing I knew, a car pulled away from the lodge."

"Jack tried to catch him in the jeep," said Maggie, "but he got away."

"Mr. Wilder," said Pudge, "don't ever do that again. Don't go chasing criminals around. You write your books and leave chasing crooks to the law. I read your books, Mr. Wilder, and I like them. I look forward to a new one. I'd hate to read about you getting yourself killed somewhere chasing crooks. I'd have to find myself another writer that appealed to me, and that wouldn't be easy. I'm a busy man. I like to stick to what I know that I like."

"Yeah, well, I don't know what got into me," said Jack. "You're right. I shouldn't have done that. Matter of fact, I'm still shaking from it all. It's not going to happen again."

"I hope not," said Maggie. "I was scared to death for you."

"Did either one of you get a good look at the car?" said Evans.

"It was a big, dark station wagon," said Maggie.

"Chevy Impala, I think," said Jackson. "About a seventy-three. Dark blue."

"What about the man? Can you describe him at all?"

"Well," Jack said, "not very well, I'm afraid. He was five-seven or five-eight, I'd say. Somewhere around there. Kind of pudgy."

Jack thought about the sheriff's name and wished that he had used a different descriptive adjective, but the thought caused only a brief pause.

"He had a round, flabby face. Thin hair. His clothes looked like he'd slept in them."

"What kind of clothes were they?"

"A business suit," said Jack. "Suit and tie, but very disheveled."

Pudge had trouble with that last word, but he wrote down something in his note pad.

"All right," he said. "Anything else comes up, you call me. No more investigating on your own. That goes for everybody here. You hear that, Dack? Inform all your guests and your hands. No more personal investigating. Whatever it is, call me."

"I'll tell them," said Hunter.

"Now, I'm going to put in a call on this Impala with the fat man in it. Maybe we'll pick him up, and I'm going to look the scene over here—pick up the flashlight and the gun. You've been wanting an investigation, Mr. Wilder. There's going to be one. This puts a whole new light on the situation. Now, you folks all go on back to bed.

If I find out anything new, or if I need you for anything, I'll let you know."

"Thank you, Sheriff," said Maggie. "Good night."

"Good night, Miz Wilder."

Maggie put an arm around Jack and turned him toward their cabin.

"I don't know if either one of us will be able to sleep at all tonight after all that's happened, but I guess we'd better try," she said.

Jack groaned as he started to walk alongside his wife.

"What's the matter, Jack?" she said. "Are you hurt?"

"No," he said. "I'm not hurt. Not really. Just bruised and a little stiff is all."

He chuckled.

"I haven't been in a fight like that for twenty years—or more."

"Well," said Maggie, "you're not a teenager anymore, and you don't need to be acting like one. We'll draw you a nice, hot bath and soak those muscles. How's that sound?"

"Sounds good."

"Jack," she said, and she smiled.

"Yeah?"

"You did make him run. You whipped him."

Breakfast was late the following morning. No one showed up at the lodge before ten. There was naturally some talk about the previous night's mysterious business, but overall the entire company was subdued. Jack and Maggie had finished eating and Jack was having a third cup of coffee when Maggie got up to excuse herself.

"I'll be back in a bit, Jack," she said. "There's something I want to do."

"Where you going?"

"I'll be back soon. You just relax and drink your coffee. Okay?"

Jack nodded, and Maggie left the room. At the table across from Jack, Tom Brock was seated between Donna Doyle and Robin Fletcher, the two romance writers, apparently having a grand time. That depressed Jack. He wasn't sure why. Dack Hunter was sitting with Vance Prescott—or rather the two Vance Prescotts—Jack couldn't decide what to call them. The door opened and Monte Clark ambled into the room and over to Hunter.

"Excuse me, boss," he said.

Hunter looked up from his conversation. Jack tried to hear what was being said without appearing to be eavesdropping.

"What is it, Monte?" said Hunter.

"Who's been riding Old Scratch? Do you know?"

"No one that I know of. You've been taking care of all that."

"Well," said Clark. "I haven't saddled Old Scratch for a week or more."

"So?"

"So Charlie just found him roaming loose along by the side of the highway—just inside the fence. He was wearing a saddle."

Hunter begged the pardon of Mr. and Mrs. Newton and left the room with Clark.

More mystery, thought Jackson. He began, in

spite of himself, to review all the facts of the
case as he knew them, beginning with Bob
Drago's drunkenness. Will McCarty had threatened to kill Drago, but that was probably just
angry talk. Drago had gone to his cabin and left
the lights on, the door open with the key in the
lock, and the curtain drawn. Someone had shot
a steel arrow into the wall of the cabin, apparently from outside and most likely using a compound bow, through the open door. Drago had
disappeared, and someone had driven Drago's
jeep, a compound bow in it, off of the mountain
road. Then the fat man had sneaked into Drago's
cabin and searched the place for—who knows
what—or tried to, before he had been interrupted by Jackson. He carried a gun. And now,
finally, though perhaps totally unrelated to all
the rest, one of the horses belonging to the
Hunter Ranch had been discovered wandering
loose and saddled when it ought not to be. None
of these pieces seemed to fit together in any way
to make any sense.

And what had happened to Bob Drago even
before all this mystery? Bob had been Jackson's
best friend. They had known each other since
their college days when both had been aspiring
young writers. Drago had always seemed to
have more talent than Jack. He had gotten his
first story published during his senior year at
college. Jack had to wait for two more years before he met with the same degree of success, and
by that time, Drago had finished two novels and
was well on the way to getting the first one published. It was Drago who had gotten Tom Brock
for an agent and then convinced Brock to take

on Jack. Drago had always been a step or two ahead of Jack in the game, and though there was a sense of rivalry between them, it had always been a friendly rivalry. Jack had always been happy for his friend's successes. Then Bob had married Sylvia, and Jack and Maggie had married, and the two couples had been nearly inseparable for several years. But when Drago became a major success, he had decided that he needed to move to New York City where, as he put it, "all the action was." They had corresponded for a short while after that, the correspondence had slowed down, then nearly stopped. Then came the news of the divorce, and Bob quit writing and calling altogether. It had been seven years, and Bob Drago, for the brief time Jack had seen him, seemed like a different man.

Jack's thoughts were interrupted when Robin Fletcher, who had been talking to Tom Brock in subdued tones, got up and walked deliberately across to sit down in the chair Maggie had vacated earlier.

"Hi," she said. "Do you mind?"

"Hi," said Jack. "No. No. Make yourself at home."

"Everyone's talking about the fight you had last night," said Robin.

Jack laughed.

"Hell," he said, "it wasn't much of a fight. We fell in the bathtub."

"The man pulled a gun on you, didn't he?"

"Yeah. Yeah. He did that. He sure did."

"You know, I usually don't read westerns, but

Tom said that I ought to read some of yours. He says they're real good."

"Yeah, well, I think so," said Jack, "but then I'm probably just a little prejudiced, you know."

"I bet they are good," said Robin. "I bet they're just fascinating."

Robin Fletcher put her hand on top of Jack's where he had it resting on the table.

"Do you have any of your books with you?" she said.

"Uh, no," said Jack. "No, I didn't bring any."

He looked at the hand on his.

"Listen," he said.

"Jack," she interrupted, "would you walk me back to my cabin? I hate to go alone."

"In the broad daylight? Nothing's going to happen out there."

"I'd just like to have your company. Okay?"

"And just what are we going to do at your cabin?" said Jack.

Robin squeezed his hand.

"Oh," she said, "we'll think of something, I'm sure. We both have good, vivid imaginations, don't we?"

Jack drew his hand out from under Robin's.

"Uh, listen, Robin," he said. "You're a lovely young woman, and you're a real temptation, but I've got more woman than I can handle already."

"Your wife?"

"My wife."

"I'm young enough to be her daughter," said Robin.

"And mine."

"Doesn't that interest you?"

"Yeah. It sure does. I'm just raring to go, but, you know, I tried it once before with a young girl. Real pretty young thing, too. She just threw herself at me, and I couldn't resist. I went for it in a big way."

"And what happened?" said Robin, leaning suggestively toward Jack.

"Maggie killed her."

"What?"

"That's right. She covered it up real good, so they never caught her."

"Oh, I don't believe you."

"Well, there's only one way I know for you to find out for sure."

"What's that?"

"Let's go to your cabin."

The door opened and Maggie came rushing back into the room. Robin got up quickly from her chair.

"I'll see you later," she said, and, as she moved back to the table with Brock and Donna Doyle, she kept her eyes nervously on Maggie Wilder.

Maggie sat down with Jack.

"I just talked to Sylvia," she said.

"I just talked to Robin."

"Robin who?"

"Robin, uh, Fletcher. The romance writer," said Jack. "Over there with Tom."

"Oh, I remember," said Maggie. "What did you talk about?"

"She wants my body."

"Well, I'm not surprised. I don't blame her, but she can't have it. What did you tell her?"

"Well, I told her that I'd just love it, but that the last time I tried it, you killed the girl."

"You didn't tell her that."

"Yes, I did."

"Well, you didn't have to tell her that I killed someone."

"It was either that or go to bed with her. I couldn't think of anything else."

"Oh, Jack."

"Sylvia who?"

"What?"

"Sylvia who? Who did you talk to?"

"Oh," said Maggie. "Sylvia. Bob Drago's Sylvia. Or his ex-Sylvia, or whatever you want to call her."

"You just talked to Sylvia?"

"I called her on the phone. Well, first I had to call Charlene, and Charlene didn't know where to find her, but she suggested that Sara Jean might know. You know, Sylvia and Sara Jean were always very close, so Charlene thought that if anyone from the old days would know where to find Sylvia it would be Sara Jean, so I called Sara Jean, and, sure enough, she had a phone number. So I called it."

"Where is she?"

"Sara Jean?"

"No. Sylvia."

"Oh, she's still in New York and living alone, but not for long."

"Not for long what?" said Jackson. "New York or alone?"

"Not alone for long. She's about to get married again."

"Oh," said Jack, "well, that's good, I guess."

"Don't you want to know who she's going to marry?"

"Why? Is it someone we know?"

The cowgirl from behind the bar came over to the table where Jack and Maggie were seated.

"Excuse me," she said, "but the sheriff is on the phone. He'd like to talk to one of you."

"Oh, yeah," said Jack. "Sure. Where . . . ?"

"You can take it right over at the bar if you like."

Jack pushed back his chair.

"My turn, babe," he said. "You just got off the phone."

He hurried over to the bar, picked up the phone, talked briefly and returned to Maggie at the table.

"He wants us to come in to his office," he said.

"What for?"

"Well, he thinks that he's got the man who was in the cabin last night."

Pudge Evans shoved himself up from his chair and stepped around the desk to greet Jackson and Maggie Wilder as they walked into his office. He shook hands with Jack and nodded politely to Maggie.

"I want to thank you folks for coming in," he said. "We caught that fellow you had a fight with. 'Course we need you to make a positive identification, but it's him. His name's Leland Krakes. He's a private investigator from New York City."

"Bob Drago lived in New York City," said Maggie.

"He may still live there," said Pudge. "We have no evidence of anything having happened to Drago. Right now, officially, he's a missing person."

"But what's a private investigator doing snooping around through Bob's things out here in Wyoming?" asked Jack.

"So far, he hasn't admitted a thing. Excuse me."

Pudge worked his way past Maggie and Jack to the door, opened it and called out.

"George," he said, "bring Krakes in here, would you?"

Then he turned to the Wilders.

"Would you folks just stand over there, please?"

"Yeah, sure," said Jack. He took Maggie by the arm and they moved over against the far wall of the office. A deputy stepped into the office with the fat man, Krakes.

"Mr. Wilder," said Pudge, "do you recognize this man?"

"Yeah, I sure do. That's the man I found in Bob Drago's cabin—the man I fought with. He drove away in an Impala station wagon. That's him."

"Thank you, Mr. Wilder. George, would you bring a couple of extra chairs in here for these folks? Thank you. Mr. Krakes, you just sit down right over there."

Krakes sat down, and George came dragging two chairs in for Jack and Maggie.

"That's all, George. Thank you," said Pudge. "Mr. Krakes, I'd like to know what it was that you were doing in that cabin. I wish you'd tell me. It would make things a whole lot easier for all of us."

"I'm a licensed private investigator," said

Krakes. "I'm working for a client, and that's all I can tell you."

"Who's your client and what's his interest in Robert Drago?"

"That's privileged information, Sheriff," said Krakes, an insolent smile on his fat lips.

"Mr. Krakes," said Pudge, "Mr. Drago has disappeared and under rather mysterious circumstances. There's the possibility of foul play. If he's been murdered or kidnapped, we'll find out sooner or later. In the meantime, we'll have you. You want to know what we'll have you for, Mr. Krakes? We'll start with trespassing. Then breaking and entering."

"I didn't break into anything," said Krakes. "The door to that cabin was standing wide open when I first got there."

"So you admit that you were in the cabin?"

"All right, I was in the cabin. Big deal. The door was open."

"Well, you'll likely have to convince a jury of that," said Pudge. "It sounds kind of fishy to me. Do you have any witnesses who will back up your story that the door was open?"

Pudge gave Jackson Wilder a warning look. Jack kept quiet. Maggie looked from Pudge to Jack, and Krakes had clamped his flabby lips shut tight.

"I didn't think so," said Pudge. He stuck a cigar in his mouth, scratched a match on his desk, and fired up. He blew out several puffs of smoke before he resumed his speech.

"Breaking and entering," he said. "Then there's attempted burglary. There's assault. Assault with intent to do bodily harm. Assault with a deadly weapon. Assault with intent to kill. Some of that, or all of it. I don't know. The prosecutor straightens out all of that. Oh, yes. There's possession of a handgun without it being registered, and carrying a concealed weapon. There's probably a few other charges, too, like maybe, speeding and attempting to run a police roadblock. Resisting arrest."

"I have a license to carry that gun," said Krakes.

"Not in Wyoming, Mr. Krakes. Not in Wyoming. In fact, your P.I. license isn't even good in this state. Now why don't you just tell me what you were up to?"

"I told you," said Krakes, "that's privileged information. My clients have to be able to trust me. If my clients couldn't trust me, I'd be out of business."

"You may be out of business anyhow, Mr. Krakes. Mr. Wilder, are you inclined to press charges of assault against Mr. Krakes here?"

"I sure am, Sheriff. You just tell me when."

"Mr. Krakes, I'm afraid that your career has already come to an end. Now if you tell me what you were up to, and if it satisfies me and Mr. and Miz Wilder here, maybe—just maybe we'll let you go on back to New York City and keep on investigating. That's the only choice you got."

Krakes slapped at his pockets. His clothes were rumpled and he was sweating.

"Have you got a cigarette?" he said. "Has anybody here got a cigarette?"

Pudge walked to the door and opened it.

"George," he called, "can you get a cigarette for Mr. Krakes here?"

George came back into the room and gave Krakes a cigarette and a light, then left again, shutting the door behind himself. Krakes drew deeply on the smoke.

"My clients are businessmen in New York City," he said. "Some time back, Bob Drago approached them about a movie deal. They don't know beans about movies. But they do know that Drago is a big-time writer. He's got lots of books. He's impressive. He's legitimate. I mean, you can go to the public library and check his books out, you know? He says that he's got connections out in Hollywood. Movie producers. They're interested in making a movie based on one of his books, but they need more bread. They, uh, they need additional investors. He feeds them a whole line of bull, which they buy, and to make a long story short, they give him a check for one hundred big ones, which he cashes."

"One hundred thousand dollars?" said Pudge.

"Yeh. Anyhow, a few months go by and he ain't done nothing. Course, they know that ain't much time for them kind of deals, but something about the way he answers their questions, or the way he don't answer them, makes them nervous. They bug him, but he still don't do nothing. They begin to think that maybe he conned them. They ask him for their money back, and he starts avoiding them like the plague. Then they hire me."

"What did they want you to do, Mr. Krakes?"

Krakes took a last long draw on his cigarette and snuffed out the butt.

"First of all, just to check up on him. I found

out that he didn't have no connection with the Hollywood producers whose names he'd been using. I found out that he hadn't had no new books for a few years and was in kind of bad shape financially. He owed a lot of dough. But I also found out that he hadn't spent the hundred thou he'd got out of my clients. At least, it don't look like he's spent it."

"So they wanted you to find out for sure whether or not he has spent the money, and if not, to get it back for them. Is that right?"

"Yeh," said Krakes. "That's it. He came out here for this trip, and I checked out his apartment in New York. He'd vacated. I figured he was planning to disappear with the money."

"What about the arrow?" said Jackson.

"What arrow?" said Krakes.

"Someone shot an arrow into Drago's cabin," said Pudge.

"Do I took like Robin Hood?"

Pudge opened the door again.

"George."

George came into the room.

"Take Mr. Krakes back to the cell, George."

"Hey," said Krakes, "what about our deal?"

"I'll let you know," said Pudge.

George took Krakes out of the office, and Pudge sat back down behind his desk.

"What do you folks think?" he said.

"Well," said Jack, "I don't know. Last week if anyone had told me that Bob Drago had tried to con someone out of a hundred thousand dollars, I'd have called him a liar. But Bob's just not the same person we used to know. He's changed.

One thing the man said that's true. Bob hadn't been writing the last few years. He was living off his past successes. That much is true."

Jackson looked at Maggie. He scratched his head. He stood up and walked across the room, turned, paced back to his chair and sat down again.

"Maggie," he said, "maybe you'd better tell him about your phone call."

"What phone call was that, Miz Wilder?" said Pudge.

"I tracked down Bob's ex-wife, Sylvia," said Maggie. "She's still in New York."

"Yes?"

"Bob changed after they moved to New York. He got mean. He beat her. I couldn't believe it at first. They used to be our best friends. He got to drinking real bad, she said, and he got meaner. He was also working, writing, less and less. Well, she finally left him and got a divorce, and that's about the time we lost track of them."

"That would fit with Krakes's story," said Pudge.

"Yeah," said Jack, "but there's one thing more."

"Sylvia's getting married again," said Maggie. "Her fiancé knows how Bob used to treat her, and he hates him for it."

Maggie paused to let that soak in.

"Another suspect," said Pudge, "if we had a crime, and if he was in the vicinity."

"Well," said Jack, "you're halfway there."

"How's that?"

"He's out at the ranch," said Maggie. "Sylvia's

engaged to marry Douglas Wayne, the adventure writer, and he's right out there at the ranch right now."

They were halfway back to the ranch before Maggie spoke. Both had been silent since leaving the sheriff's office. They were each thinking their own thoughts about what they had heard of Bob Drago from Sylvia and from Leland Krakes. When Maggie finally broke the silence, Jack didn't hear her for the noise of the jeep. She repeated herself, this time in a louder voice and leaning over toward his ear.

"Jack."

"Yeah?"

"Sylvia said something else."

"What'd she say?"

"Sylvia said that she thought that Bob had been all right as long as it was just you and him."

"What? What do you mean?"

"As long as he was in Oklahoma and he was only just competing with you, he was okay."

Jack furrowed his brow.

"But when they got to New York, she said, the competition was just too much for him. That's when he started drinking, and that's when he started to get mean."

"Competition?" said Jack. "What competition? There was no competition between me and Bob."

But he knew even as he denied it that there had been.

Chapter Five

SHERMAN POSTOAK STOPPED his '69 GMC pickup in the road and shut off the engine. He looked across the cab out the window on the passenger's side and into the woeful eyes of Ajax, whose head was sticking through the hogwire fence. Ajax bleated. Sherman expelled a long and tired sigh. He opened the door and crawled out of the pickup, his feet kicking up dust puffs as he walked around to the fence. He groaned as he squatted down in front of the wretched goat.

"I don't know why Jack and Maggie haven't ate you for dinner long time ago," he said, as he gripped the two horns and twisted the goat's head to shove it back through the fence. Once free, Ajax ran bleating joyfully for tall grass. Sherman walked over to the mailbox and emptied it of its contents. He went back to the pickup, tossed the mail in on the seat and climbed back in behind the wheel. He started the engine, dropped the lever down into first and turned into the driveway headed for the house.

Parked in front of the house, Sherman lit a cigarette and smoked it casually. He was in no hurry to get back home, and things were real peaceful and quiet at the Wilders' place. With Ajax out of the fence, there was really nothing to distract Sherman from his own relaxation. It was a nice place. The driveway was long enough that the house sat well back from the road, and the road wasn't much more than a driveway ei-

ther. It led to a couple of other houses, but that
was all. The house and a small barn opposite it
on the other side of the driveway were nestled in
a quiet little clearing in the woods, and just beyond the end of the driveway, the hills rose
sharply. It was a nice spot, and Sherman was
happy for his friends. At the moment, though, he
was even happier for himself. It was a place of
quiet respite from the chaos of his own home,
where at that very moment a brother and two
sisters were visiting with their families. *Must be
twenty kids over there,* he thought with smug satisfaction at being away. He took the last drag
from his cigarette and tossed it away into the
dirt, then he picked up the stack of mail from
the pickup seat. Fingering his way through it, he
muttered half aloud to himself.

"Bills, bills, junk mail. Hmm. Looks like a roy-
alty check. Bills, bills, bills."

He opened the door of the pickup and stepped
out, leaving the mail on the seat. Then he withdrew his billfold from his rear pocket, opened it
and carefully withdrew a key which he had
tucked into one of the tiny compartments. He
stuck the billfold back into his pocket, picked up
the stack of mail and went to the front door of
the Wilders' house. He unlocked the door,
opened it and stepped inside. Just as he tossed
the mail on top of the pile already there on a
table beside the door, he heard a scurry followed by the sound of a door being opened and
then slamming shut again. He felt his heart
jump in his chest. He started toward the kitchen
and the back door, then realized that would be
futile and ran out the front door. Just as he

rounded the corner of the house heading for the
back, a figure, moving fast, loomed up before
him, thrust out two open palms and hit him in
the chest on the run. Sherman flew backward
and landed flat. The fall stunned him momentarily, knocked all the breath out of him. As
soon as he was able, he struggled to his feet and
trotted after the man, but it was too late. Whoever it was had disappeared into the woods behind the small barn.

Jackson Wilder held the horseshoe up in front
of his face and carefully sighted. He let the
weight of the shoe carry his arm back on a
smooth downswing, then flung the piece of iron
through the air. It struck dirt with a dull thud,
flipped over and leaned against the post.

"Ha, ha, I got a leaner there," he said.

Maggie danced around the post with the
leaner on it.

"Good shot, Jack," she said. "Show them how
this game is played in Oklahoma."

Joyce Newton stepped up where Jackson had
been. She held a horseshoe out in front of her at
arm's length, stretched her arm out behind her
and flung the shoe with all her might. It made an
awkward flight, struck the grass off to the side of
the post and skittered into the post knocking
Jack's leaner away.

"Damn," said Jack.

"That's the spirit," shouted Charles Newton
from the other end of the playing field.

"Well, Maggie," said Jack, "it's up to you."

Maggie picked up a horseshoe just as Dack
Hunter stepped around the corner of the lodge.

"Mr. Wilder," he said, "I've got a phone call for you inside. Long distance."

"Well," said Jack, "I guess you guys win by default. How lucky can you get?"

"You're not getting away with that," said Charles Newton. "We'll wait this game for you. Lucky, my eye."

"I better take that phone call," said Jack, and he fell in step with Hunter on his way back into the lodge. As they entered the building, Hunter pointed to a room off to one side.

"You can take that in my office, if you like," he said.

Jack stepped inside the office and picked up the phone.

"Hello."

"Jack?"

"Yeah, this is Jack Wilder."

"Jack, I caught somebody in your house."

"Sherman?"

"Yeah."

"You say you caught someone in the house?"

"Well," said Sherman, "I didn't exactly catch him. I didn't know he was there. I went in the front door and he went out the back. I ran around the house from the front and ran smack into him. He knocked me down and got away."

"Sherm, are you all right? Did he hurt you?"

"No, I'm okay. Just knocked the wind out of me is all. I wish I'd have caught him. I didn't even get a good look at him."

"Hell, Sherman, I'm glad you didn't catch him. You damn fool, you might have gotten yourself killed. Anything like that ever happens again, don't even try to stop them."

Jack realized that he was sounding like Pudge Evans, who had given him a similar stern warning not long ago. He felt a bit foolish, but he also felt like he understood Pudge a little better.

"Are you sure you're okay?" he said.

"Yeah. Yeah. Don't worry about me. I'm getting old but I'm still tough. I couldn't see that anything was missing. I called the sheriff, and me and him looked around. Couldn't really find nothing, but I thought I'd ought to call and let you know."

"Well, I appreciate that, Sherman. Where are you calling from?"

"I'm in your house. The sheriff just left."

"Okay. Now you be careful around there until we get back. It was probably just a prowler, and he probably won't be back, but be careful. Stay safe, buddy, you hear me?"

"Don't worry. Everything's okay here. Nothing's missing. Nothing broke."

"How'd he get in the house?"

"Damned if we could tell. Sheriff figured he probably used a credit card on the door lock. Something like that. You ought to get a better lock, you know? You get pretty high-quality prowlers around here."

"What do you mean?"

"Carrying credit cards."

"Oh. Yeah. I suppose so. Sherman?"

"Yeah?"

"How's Ajax getting along?"

"He sticks his head in the damn fence every day. That sorry goat. Why don't you let me butcher him for you while you're up there in Wyoming?"

"Are you kidding? You know what Maggie'd do to both of us if I let you do that?"

"Well, anyhow, he's okay, long as I push his head back through the fence once a day. It's that other one you ought to be asking about."

"Crackerjacks?"

"Yeah, that little female."

"Why? What's wrong with her?"

"She's pregnant."

"By Ajax?"

"Ain't no one else in there to blame it on, Jackson."

"Oh, no," said Jackson. "I don't know how I'm going to break this news to Maggie."

"What's wrong with a pregnant goat? You'll just have some little ones around the place. Turn it into a business."

"Aw, man, Sherman, Ajax is her brother."

Jackson heard the front door of the lodge open and glanced over his shoulder to see Pudge Evans striding in.

"Hey, buddy," he said into the phone, "I'm going to have to run. You sure everything's okay now?"

"Everything's fine."

"Okay, then. You call again if you need to, and we'll see you in a few days, okay? Thanks for everything, buddy. Be seeing you. Goodbye."

Jack hung up the phone and followed Pudge Evans into The Old Corral. Since Jack had broken up the game of horseshoes, the remaining players had all adjourned to that watering spot, too. As Jack stepped into the room, Pudge had just taken a prominent position beside the bar and turned to face the room.

"Dack," he said, "is everybody in here?"

Hunter looked around the room.

"I think so, Pudge," he said. "Mr. Brock?"

"Yes," said Tom Brock. "We're all here. What's this all about?"

"Good," said Pudge. "I want to talk about this Drago case. We're in the middle of a full-scale investigation here, although to be perfectly honest with you, we don't know exactly what it is we're investigating."

Will McCarty stood up and headed for the bar.

"I think I need a drink," he said.

"That's probably not a bad idea," said Pudge. "This is liable to take a while, so all of you folks get yourselves a drink, whatever you need, so you can settle back and take it. I'll wait a minute here before I get started."

Dack Hunter snapped his fingers at the cowgirl behind the bar, then got up to help her fill orders. Maggie got a small glass of white wine. Jack had coffee. At the bar Pudge Evans had a giant glass of lemonade. As the cowgirl left the table where Jack and Maggie sat, Maggie took advantage of the delay in the proceedings to question Jackson.

"Jack," she said, "who called?"

"What?"

"What was your phone call?"

"Oh. Oh, that was Sherman."

"Sherman?"

"Yeah."

"What did he call for? Is everything all right at home?"

"Well, I don't know," said Jack. "He had some bad news."

"What is it?"

"Maggie, I don't know how to tell you this, but your damn goat is guilty of incest."

"What?"

"Crackerjacks is pregnant."

"She is?"

Maggie was not upset at the news of Crackerjacks's pregnancy. On the contrary, she seemed rather pleased at the thought. Jack shook his head.

"Yeah," he said. "Ajax did it. Her own brother."

"Oh, silly," said Maggie, "goats don't know any better. You don't call it that with goats."

"Well, it's not very nice. I don't think it's very nice of him. I'm going to have to have a talk with him when we get back. I guess that's where the bard got that one line, 'as prime as goats.' You know that one?"

"Oh, Jackson. Is that what Sherman called to tell you? Really?"

"That's what he told me."

"But was that all he told you?"

"Uh, there was one other thing."

"Well, are you going to tell me or do I have to wring your neck?"

"He caught a prowler in the house this morning."

"In our house?"

"Yeah."

"Well, for God's sake, Jack, what happened?"

"Shh. Hush, babe. Pudge is getting ready to do his thing here."

"Jack."

"Be still now. I'll tell you all about it after a while. Everything's okay. Trust me."

Everyone in the room had been served by this time, and Pudge Evans was indeed strutting before the bar and clearing his throat. Maggie, with some difficulty, quieted herself and settled back in her chair, but not until she had given Jackson a hard and threatening look.

"Now," said Pudge, "before we go any farther, let's just review the facts of this case so we're all together on the whole thing. The first night you people were here at the Hunter Ranch, Mr. Robert Drago, one of your number, got himself real tanked up in here and among other things poured a drink on Mr. McCarty there. Immediately thereafter Mr. McCarty was heard to threaten the life of Mr. Drago."

"Hey, wait a minute," said McCarty.

"Just hold on there, Mr. McCarty," said Pudge. "I'm talking. You can take a turn in a bit if you really want to. Mr. McCarty was heard to threaten the life of Mr. Drago. Mr. Drago left the bar and no one that we know of has seen him since. Sometime during that same night, someone shot an arrow into the wall of Mr. Drago's cabin, using a compound bow, and the next day the jeep that had been assigned to Mr. Drago was found overturned off the mountain road with a compound bow underneath it. The lights were on in Mr. Drago's room. The curtains were drawn, that is, they were open, and the door was open. Mr. and Miz Wilder saw it like that when they went to bed that night Mr. Drago disappeared. We found it still like that the next day. Since then a private investigator from New York

City was caught in the Drago cabin rummaging through the drawers. Mr. Wilder confronted him and struggled with him. The intruder pulled a gun on Mr. Wilder, who is lucky that he didn't get himself killed. My deputies apprehended the man later the same night. He's still in custody. The man's name is Krakes."

Pudge paused and took a long drink of lemonade. Everyone in the room was quiet, and Pudge could detect no hint of recognition on anyone's part at the mention of the name of Leland Krakes. He put his big glass down on the bar.

"Now Krakes said that he was working for some businessmen in New York City," he continued, "that Drago had swindled out of a large sum of money—one hundred thousand dollars, to be exact. He had conned them with some sort of story about a movie deal. These men want their money back. We did some checking on Krakes and on Drago with the New York City police, and the story seems to check out. Now is everybody with me?"

He paused and took another long drink of lemonade. No one else spoke.

"Now, we've got two deadly weapons involved in this deal, a missing person and a missing one hundred thousand dollars. We've also got an overturned jeep. I think that we have cause here for serious concern. Now, Mr. McCarty, it's your turn."

"What do you want me to say?" said McCarty.

"You were pretty anxious to say something a minute ago," said Pudge.

McCarty had apparently reconsidered as

Pudge had told the whole story. He took a drink from his scotch and soda.

"You threatened Mr. Drago's life in the presence of witnesses," Pudge said.

"Hey," said McCarty, standing up, "I was mad. Okay? People say all kinds of things when they're mad. The sot had just poured a drink all over my head, and I said I ought to kill him. What I really wanted to do was to just beat the living daylights out of him."

"I can understand what you're saying," said the sheriff. "It is easy to say something you don't mean in the heat of anger. That's very true. You know, the sheriff's office hasn't been idle these few days. We've been catching up on our reading."

There were some murmurs around the room.

"That's right," said Pudge. "Take this book here for instance."

Pudge held up a hardcover western novel for all to see.

"I ain't read the book yet," he said. "Just the, uh, what do you call it? The dust jacket? Yeah. The dust jacket. Can all of you see this?"

McCarty could, and he sat stiffly in his chair staring at the book in the sheriff's hand.

"Well," Pudge went on, "let me read to you. This here is a western novel called *The Cow Creek Forty*, and it was written by Mr. McCarty here. I do intend to read this book as soon as I get the time, Mr. McCarty. *The Cow Creek Forty*. That's a real catchy title. I want to find out what it means. Anyhow, here's what it says about Mr. McCarty on the dust jacket: *The Cow Creek Forty* is Will McCarty's sixth novel of the west. Though an easterner, McCarty has had a lifelong love affair with the west, having grown up on the novels of such greats as Max Brand, Luke Short, and Nelson Nye. McCarty is an accomplished horseman, having ridden in numerous shows on the East Coast, and is a world champion archer in the compound bow class.' That's a real nice picture of you on there, Mr. McCarty."

There were loud murmurs and a few astonished outcries.

"That's right," Pudge said, "the compound bow."

The room became silent. McCarty stared at Pudge Evans. He was shaking with fear and panic. He drained his drink, put down the glass and leaned for a moment on the table.

"All right," he said. "All right. I fired the arrow. I did that. But that's all I did. I didn't do anything to Drago. I followed him out of the bar that night and saw him drop the keys to the jeep. He was so drunk that he couldn't find them in the dark, so he just walked on back to his cabin. I followed him. I saw that he didn't even get the door shut or turn the lights out, so I hurried on over to my cabin, got the bow and a couple of arrows, went back out and shot the arrow into the wall. I just wanted to throw a scare into him —to get even a little—to maybe scare him into leaving. That's all. And maybe it worked. Maybe nothing's happened to him at all. Maybe he just ran off."

"Without his clothes?" said Pudge.

"I don't know. I don't know," said McCarty coming up out of his chair. "I swear to God that's all I did."

"You said two arrows, Mr. McCarty. What did you do with the second one?"

"I tossed it into Drago's jeep with the bow."

"Wait a minute," said Jackson Wilder, standing up from his seat. "Wait a minute."

Pudge Evans looked at Jack.

"Yes, Mr. Wilder?" he said.

"Excuse me," said Jack. "I'm sorry to interrupt, but can I ask a question?"

"By all means, Mr. Wilder," said Pudge. "Ask your question."

"Well, uh, I guess maybe it's not a question after all. It's more of an observation. We've been assuming that Bob drove the jeep off the road, right? But McCarty just said that Bob lost the keys and walked back to his cabin."

"I picked them up," said McCarty.

"What did you do with them after that?" asked the sheriff.

"I put them in the jeep."

Pudge Evans cleared his throat loudly, paced a few steps along the bar and scratched his head.

"Mr. McCarty," he said, "I'm going to ask you to go down to my office with me after awhile when we get through here and make a formal statement to the effect of all that you've told us here today. Did you see Mr. Drago in the cabin when you shot that arrow?"

"Yeah. Yeah, he was in there."

"Then all we have is your word that you didn't aim at him. That weapon of yours is designed to kill. You could be charged with attempted murder, Mr. McCarty, and you may be before we're through here. For now just sit down."

McCarty sat down. He was still shaking.

"Oh, one other thing, Mr. McCarty," said Pudge. "We only found the bow with the jeep. We didn't find that second arrow."

"I don't know anything about that. I told you, I put it in the jeep."

"You didn't drive the jeep anywhere?"

"No, I didn't. I did just what I've told you and nothing more."

Pudge turned to the cowgirl behind the bar.

"Miss," he said, "would you kindly get Mr. McCarty another drink? I believe he needs it pretty bad."

While the cowgirl mixed a drink and took it over to McCarty, Pudge drained his giant-sized glass of lemonade.

"Anybody else need a refill?" he asked.

"You mean there's more?" asked Douglas Wayne.

The cowgirl moved around the tables taking orders quietly.

"More what, Mr. Wayne?" said Pudge.

"You're going to keep us here longer?"

"There's more, Mr. Wayne. Why don't you tell us just exactly what it is you've got against Robert Drago?"

"What are you talking about?"

"Is it true that you're engaged to be married?"

Wayne's face went white.

"You're engaged to marry the former Miz Robert Drago. Isn't that true?"

"Yes," said Wayne. "It's true, and I know what you're driving at. It's true that I hate Robert Drago about as much as I could hate anyone. Sylvia is a wonderful woman, and he treated her like . . ."

"Like what, Mr. Wayne?"

"Never mind. I don't want to talk about it. I don't even like to think about the things he did to her. Since you brought it up, let me tell you something. I didn't kill him. But he sure deserved killing, and if it turns out that somebody did kill him, I'll be glad of it, and I'm not ashamed to admit it. Yes, I have a motive. Who doesn't who knows Bob Drago? But I didn't do it. So good luck to you, Sheriff. Do your worst."

Pudge nodded his head slowly, taking it all in. The cowgirl put a full giant lemonade on the bar beside him, and he took a long gulp.

"Mr. Brock," he said.

Brock stiffened.

"Yes, Sheriff?"

"Mr. Brock, you are Robert Drago's literary agent. Is that correct?"

"That's right," said Brock. "I represent all of the authors here. The whole purpose of this gathering was to celebrate a particularly successful year. An agency, by that I mean the agent and all his clients, is like a family. I invited my clients to spend this time with me at the Hunter Ranch. It's my treat. It's my way of saying 'thank you' to all my writers who are responsible for the success of the year."

"Was Robert Drago responsible for any of that success?"

"Robert Drago is one of my clients," said Brock.

"I understand that Drago hasn't written anything for several years. Is that correct?"

"Robert Drago's books were big successes. Several of them are still in print and still selling well. As Drago's agent, I receive ten percent of the royalties. Yes, Robert was responsible for part of the success of the past year."

"Mr. Brock," said Pudge, "excuse my ignorance. I don't know anything about this literary business. As Robert Drago's literary agent, do you receive ten percent of everything he makes? I mean, if Drago, or any of your clients for that matter, went out and sold something on his own, made the deal without you, do you still get your cut?"

"Why, yes," said Brock. "That's a part of the agreement we sign."

"Did you receive ten percent of the one hundred thousand dollars Mr. Drago is alleged to have been paid by the clients of Leland Krakes for some kind of movie deal?"

Brock was silent. He saw that the sly old country sheriff had tricked him into exposing his own motive. He would now be another suspect. He clutched his drink glass tightly and clenched his teeth.

"Mr. Brock?"

"No," said Brock. "No, I didn't."

"Then one might say that Mr. Drago owed you ten thousand dollars. In fact, one might go so far as to say that Mr. Drago had cheated you out of ten thousand dollars. Not an insubstantial sum of money. Would you say so?"

"I didn't know about that money," said Brock. "If Bob got that money from someone for screenwriting, then I should have received my percentage."

"We have only your word that you didn't know about the deal, Mr. Brock."

"I'm not lying," shouted Brock.

"Take it easy," said Pudge. "No one said you were. I'm only dealing in factual information here."

He took a cigar out of his pocket and lit it.

"I hope that you people see what we're up against here," he said. "We've had a man disappear under very mysterious circumstances. We've got more suspects with good, strong motives than we know what to do with. And we've got no crime. I don't know if this little talk did any of you any good or not. I thought that it might do me some good, but I don't know if it even did that. I don't think that I have any legal means of detaining you folks whenever you're ready to leave the state, but I do intend to keep track of your whereabouts until this thing is finally all cleared up one way or another, and I hope that we don't hear of any more strange goings-on out here at the ranch. Mr. McCarty, I still want that formal statement from you."

"Sheriff," said Jackson, "what do you do now?"

"Mr. Wilder," said Pudge, "first thing in the morning, starting where that jeep went off the road, I'm going to search this whole countryside. I wouldn't object to any volunteer help either on that job."

Pudge Evans took Will McCarty with him and left the ranch, and the crowd in The Old Corral, for the most part, sat still and silent. They tried not even to look at one another. The silence was finally broken when old Sourdough opened the door and stepped into the room. He looked around, perplexed.

"What the hell's wrong in here?" he said. "It's like a funeral. Did somebody die and I didn't get told about it?"

Sourdough's questions went without answers, and he shrugged his shoulders, sauntered over to the bar and ordered a beer. His first long sip left foam clinging to his whiskers. He looked up at the cowgirl behind the bar who had served him the beer.

"Hey, girlie," he said, "what's going on here anyhow?"

"The sheriff just left," said the cowgirl, non-committally.

"Who? Old Pudge? So? What'd he do before he left? Let a big fart?"

The cowgirl turned red in the face, and Dack Hunter got up and walked over to the bar.

"Sourdough," he said. "Watch your language. Pudge was here on official business."

"So what are all the long faces for? Did they find that writer feller?"

"No. Drago hasn't been found. But, well, Pudge took Will McCarty in with him. I don't think he's arrested him—just took him in to get a statement—but it doesn't look good for Will. He admitted shooting the arrow into the cabin."

"Dack," said Sourdough, "I told you whenever you said there was a bunch of writers coming up here, I told you they'd be a weird bunch. You remember? I told you that. Writers. A bunch of weirdos."

"Keep your voice down, you old goat."

"Well, now," said Sourdough, "what'd I say?"

"Just shut up," said Hunter through clenched teeth.

Sourdough shrugged his shoulders and took another long sip of his beer.

"Do you think Will did it?" said Myrna Keck.

"Did what, Myrna?" said Tom Brock with exasperation in his voice. "Did what? Did you hear the sheriff? He said we've got no crime."

"I know that, Tom, but we all know that something's happened to Drago. He's probably been killed and his body just hasn't turned up yet."

"Bodies don't just turn up."

"Well, you know what I mean."

"Myrna, nothing's happened. At least, that's the way I'm going to look at it until someone comes up with some proof of something. You got that? Nothing's happened."

"You don't have to talk to me like I'm a dummy or something. I can understand you. I understand plain English."

"What do you think, Donna?" said Robin Fletcher.

Donna Doyle put her chin in her hand and stared off across the room.

"Well," she said, "I think somebody here probably knocked him off. I think that Jack Wilder was on the right track from the start. The problem is figuring out who did it. I don't think Will did it. Do you?"

"Well, who then?"

"It could be almost anybody. Nobody liked the little rat. He tried to put the make on me one day at Tom's office. I almost got drunk smelling his breath. I could have pushed him down the stairs and killed him that day. I thought about it."

"You didn't do it, did you?" said Robin, a sly grin on her face.

"No. No such luck."

Vance Prescott had a notepad out on the table before them, and Charles was writing in it.

"What will we call Tom?" said Joyce.

"It's so difficult," said Charles. "Knowing Tom, one thinks of him as a natural Tom, you know? We have to think of him as another character. Put Tom out of mind. It's not going to be Tom, really, just an agent. It could be anyone."

"A George."

"No, I don't like George."

"A Willard."

"No. No. No, but Willard we can use, I think. Willard should be the name of that private eye, you know, what's his name? Krakes. We'll change Krakes to Willard—Willard—Willard McGraw. McGraw is a private-eye name if there ever was one, and Willard goes well with that. Don't you think?"

"Yes, I like it," said Joyce.

"Good," said Charles. "Will we use Jack Wilder?"

"Well, I think we need him, don't you? After all, he's the old friend. The only one with anything good to say about the victim. I'm not sure that we need Maggie, though."

"Is Jack the hero? Or the sheriff?"

"I don't like a Wyoming sheriff for our hero, Charles. That's not our style."

"Then it's got to be Jack, and that's all the

more reason for not using Maggie. We'll want a single, eligible bachelor for a hero. Someone we might be able to use again."

"Wait a minute," said Joyce. "What about us?"

"Us?"

"A husband-and-wife team of mystery writers suddenly thrown into a situation where they're forced to become detectives for real. The sheriff is incompetent. It's a sure winner. Dude ranch setting."

"What will we call ourselves?"

"You know, Jack," said Maggie, breaking the silence they had been sitting in for some minutes, "there's a peculiar thing about this case."

"Seems to me like the whole thing is peculiar," said Jack.

"Well, yes, but I mean something more particular. Listen to this. Like Pudge said, we have more suspects than we know what to do with. Almost everyone seems to have a motive."

"Yeah."

"So I asked myself, of all those with motives, who has the most to gain if Bob was killed?"

"And what's the answer?"

"No one. That's what's peculiar. No one has anything to gain with Bob's death. All the motives are just revenge or hate or something like that. Revenge for the pouring of the drink on Will McCarty's head. Revenge for the way Bob treated Sylvia. Tom wouldn't get his ten thousand dollars if Bob were to be killed—only revenge for having been cheated out of it. No one has anything to gain."

"If Bob really did swindle all that money out

of Krakes's clients, and if he really hasn't spent it, they would have that to gain. Get their money back."

"But they wouldn't have him killed until they had the money. And Krakes apparently didn't find it."

"You're right. It's a puzzle," said Jack. He looked up to see John Garretson and Vaughan Hacker approaching the table. "Oh, hi, boys. Pull up a chair."

"We sure got more than we counted on for this trip," said Garretson. "Can I buy you guys a drink?"

"Yeah," said Hacker, "I'll have a refill."

He turned toward the bar and held his empty glass high over his head to get the attention of the cowgirl. She caught his gesture and hustled out from behind the bar.

"Damn," said Garretson, "I wasn't talking to you. How about it, Jack? Maggie?"

"Well," said Maggie, "I guess I could have one more glass of wine."

Jack lifted his coffee cup slightly off the saucer.

"I'll just have a refill of this," he said.

"You could lace it a little with some Irish whiskey," said Garretson.

"No, thanks."

The waitress took the orders and left again to fill them.

"Well," said Garretson, "you think this Sheriff Evans will ever get to the bottom of all this?"

"I don't know," said Jack. "It's a puzzle. That's for sure. He's a good man, though, that sheriff. A good man."

"You think so?"

"He's a good man."

"Well, anyhow," said Hacker, "you finally got your way, Jack."

"What's that? What do you mean?"

"Hell, at first, we all thought that you were full of baloney. We all thought that old Bob was just off drunk somewhere, but now with arrows and guns and wrecked jeeps and that fight you had and a missing hundred grand, everybody's all excited and the sheriff's conducting a full-scale investigation."

"Oh, I see. Yeah. I guess I did get my way, didn't I?"

The cowgirl showed up just then and served the drinks around.

It had been a long day. Jack and Maggie excused themselves early and left the lodge to walk back to their cabin. It was dark outside, and the night air was crisp with a slight mountain chill in the breeze. The sky was a stargazer's delight. As they ambled toward the cabin, Jack took Maggie's hand in his.

"Let's just walk," said Maggie.

"Walk along in the dark and hold hands?"

"Um-hum."

"Just like when we were a couple of college kids?"

"Just like."

"Yeah," said Jack. "That was how many years ago?"

"Oh, I don't think you really want to know," said Maggie. "Your hair was black then."

"Did you like me better with black hair?"

Maggie hugged Jack's arm to her side.

"I like you just a little bit better each year," she said.

"Really?"

"Yes. Really."

"No matter what happens to my hair?"

"No matter."

"What if it all fell out?"

"Oh, I don't know about that. I think you'd be ugly with a bald head."

"Yeah, I would be. I could get myself a collection of wigs, though. All different styles, you know? Different colors. I could change every now and then so you wouldn't get tired of me."

They had aimlessly changed the direction of their walk and wound up, not at the cabin, but at the rail fence that ran alongside the mountain road. Jack leaned his elbows on the rail, and Maggie put an arm around his shoulder.

"It's a lovely night," she said.

"Yeah," said Jack. "It really is. The sky looks so much bigger up here than down home. That doesn't make sense, does it?"

"That's why they call it, the Big Sky Country."

"No, babe, that's Montana."

Maggie pointed off over the valley.

"Well, Montana's just over there."

Jack took hold of her wrist and turned her arm just a bit so that she was pointing in a slightly different direction.

"Over there," he said.

"Well, whatever. It's still the same sky. Some of Montana's sky has leaked over this way, and that's why it looks so big."

Jack straightened up from where he had been leaning on the rail. He put a hand on each of Maggie's shoulders and looked her in the eyes with a stern and serious expression on his face.

"You know, babe," he said, "I like you a hell of a lot. I really do."

He kissed her, long and lovingly, then held her close to his chest, breathing in the scent of her hair. He took a deep breath and let out a long sigh.

"Let's go to bed, huh?" he said.

He left one arm around her as they began the walk toward the cabin.

"Are we going to join that search in the morning, Jack?" said Maggie.

"Well, I figured I would," he said.

"Then I will, too. I can ride as good as you."

"Better," said Jack. "Hell, you're an old barrel racer, you are. They don't get much better than that. Yeah, well, I guess we'll have to roll out kind of early in the morning."

As they reached the cabin and stepped inside, Jack flipped on the light switch. He closed the door behind them and latched it.

"Jack," said Maggie, "what do you think we'll find out there?"

Jack dropped into the big easy chair that sat against the wall by the picture window. He pulled off a boot and dropped it to the floor. Then he looked up at Maggie.

"I don't know," he said. "I'm not even sure what I hope we find. In a way, I hope we don't find anything. I'm afraid of what it might be. In another way, I think I'd welcome almost anything that would clear this mess up once and for all. I hate to say it."

"I know what you mean," said Maggie, running a hand through his hair. "Let's try not to think about it any more until morning."

Chapter Six

IT WAS 6:00 A.M. when the nasal-sounding buzzer on the alarm clock began to bleat. Jack Wilder stirred in his sleep and silently cursed Ajax. His dream images changed, and he saw the goat's head sticking through the hogwire fence. He hated to get himself up and out of bed to go to the rescue. "Damn that goat," he said, perhaps aloud, perhaps only in his dream. Maggie reached out in the darkness to fumble for the offending machine and silence it. She snuggled back into her pillow, but, by then half-awake, recalled the reason she had set the clock the night before to go off so early. She sat up and rubbed her eyes, then reached for the bedside lamp and snapped it on. The sudden brightness was initially painful.

"Jack," she said.

Jack mumbled something incoherent and rolled over in the bed. Maggie leaned across the

bed and over him. She kissed him on the cheek
and on the ear.

"Wake up," she said. "We have to get out early
this morning. Remember?"

Jack finally came awake. He reached out and
pulled Maggie down close to him.

"Good morning, love," he said. "Um. This is a
hell of a nice way to wake up in the morning. I
still love you."

"You sure?"

"I'm sure."

"Good. But we do have to get up and get going
this morning."

"Oh. Oh, yeah. Pudge this morning," said Jack.
"Good old Pudge."

In the bathroom, Jack wet his shaving brush
and dipped it into the mug to stir up a lather.
Then he daubed the thick suds on his face, put
down the mug and brush, and picked up an old,
well-used straight razor. An ancient razor strop
was hanging on a hook that he had found conve-
nient there in the bathroom. Taking up the bottom end of the strop, he whisked the razor several times back and forth across it before
beginning to shave. Jack had tried an electric
razor once, one guaranteed to shave him closer
than a blade, and he hadn't liked it. He had told
Maggie that it was like running a lawn mower
over his face. He preferred the old razor and its
accompanying paraphernalia that had all be-
longed to his grandfather, Grandpa Wilder. He
had given the electric thing to Sherman Postoak,
who had been delighted with it and had used it
every morning since then. The modern contrap-

tion had also deprived Jack of what was to him, apparently, an important early-morning ritual.

Scraping off his stubble with the old razor made him think of Grandpa Wilder. He wondered what the old man might have done in a situation like this. One thing he knew for sure. If Grandpa Wilder were here right now getting ready to ride out on this search, he'd already have strapped on his old .38. That was certain. And the other night, when that joker from New York, what was his name, Krakes—the other night when Krakes had reached under his coat, if he'd been facing Grandpa Wilder, he wouldn't be alive today to sit in a cell in Pudge Evans's jailhouse. Grandpa Wilder would have pulled his .38 and blown Krakes away. That's what Grandpa Wilder would have done. Jack often wished that he could be more like the old man, but the times were so changed that, of course, people had to change with them. But it was nice to remember Grandpa Wilder, and it was always interesting to speculate as to what he might have done in a given contemporary situation.

Ten riders had gathered along the rim on the mountain road just where the jeep had gone over the side. Sheriff Pudge Evans and his deputy, George, were in the lead. The ranch owner, Hunter, and his top hand, Monte Clark, were along, and in their company rode the old cook, Sourdough, who had driven the chuckwagon on the excursion the day the jeep had been discovered. Sourdough was a man who had obviously been carefully chosen for his role. He had the appearance of a man much older than his actual years, probably due to a carefully cultivated scruffy, gray beard and purposefully baggy clothes. His whole appearance was topped off by an ancient battered hat. Sourdough was just what all the tourists would expect to see in a ranch cook, and he played the part well. Of the writer-guests, only Vaughan Hacker, John Garretson and Will McCarty joined the Wilders on the search. Jack again rode the Appaloosa and Maggie the pinto.

Above the riders the mountains rose sharply, their tops peaked with white. Below, the mountains quickly assumed the lesser stature of foothills, gradually sloping into an expansive valley that meandered on over to the highway. The valley was squared off on one end by the long driveway into the ranch from the highway, but off to the right of the riders as they looked down into the valley, there was virtually no end to the wilderness. The tall grass billowed like ocean waves across the valley floor, which was randomly spotted by patches of yellow wildflowers and huge flat rocks that appeared to have been set here and there by some deliberate giant hand.

Pudge Evans turned his horse to face the rest of the riders.

"Listen up, please," he said. "In just a minute, we're going to ride on ahead to a place where we can get down from the road to that shelf the jeep is on. The shelf runs almost the length of this valley, and you can get down into the valley from off the shelf at most any point without too much trouble. Getting to the shelf from here, though, is a different story. There's only this one place on up here ahead, and we'll have to ride down single file. We'll let Mr. Hunter and Monte lead the way for us.

"Now what we want to do is, we want to search this whole area starting from the point where we ride down clear back to the ranch road, all the way from the ledge out to the highway. Mr. Hunter and Monte, being in the lead, will ride all the way down to the ranch road. Then Sourdough. Mr. and Miz Wilder, why don't you go next? Then me and George, McCarty, and then you two."

Pudge nodded toward Hacker and Garretson.

"That means that when you, Mr. Garretson, get down to the ledge, you don't need to ride along it at all. Go right on down into the valley and start working your way out toward the highway. But if you get down to the ledge before Mr. Hunter has reached the other end, wait until Mr. Hunter starts down so we'll all move forward together. We'll be spread out some, but we ought to be able to hear each other holler in case anyone finds anything or runs into any kind of trouble. Any questions?"

"Yeah," said Garretson. "Just what are we looking for?"

"I don't know, Mr. Garretson," said Pudge. "You find anything interesting, you just holler. Okay?"

Garretson nodded, and Pudge looked at Hunter.

"Mr. Hunter," he said, "you want to lead on?"

Hunter urged his horse forward along the mountain road, and the others fell in behind in the order assigned by the sheriff. Soon they had reached the spot where Monte Clark had led

Jackson down the hillside earlier in the week, and Hunter eased his mount onto the treacherous path. It took a while before the entire search party was spread out along the ledge and Garretson at one end and Hunter at the other were ready to begin moving on down into the valley. Dack Hunter was practically riding fence at his end. The others were more or less evenly spaced out between Hunter and Garretson. Once down in the rolling prairie grass, Pudge Evans eased himself over near his deputy.

"George," he said, "that fella off to your right is Will McCarty. He's the archer I told you about. I'm kind of surprised to see him join the search this morning. Keep your eye on him, will you?"

"Sure, Pudge," said George.

As the sun rose higher in the sky, and the morning grew older, the heat on the valley floor grew more intense. The sense of the cool prairie breezes causing the tall grass to rise and swell gave over to the more immediate and realistic sense of the grass as a hot, dusty, sticky haven for millions of insects. Jack Wilder looked in the direction of his wife.

"Boy," he said, "it sure takes a lot longer to cross this valley than it looked like it would from up above."

"Yes, it does," said Maggie.

They rode on for a few more moments in silence, combing the grass with their eyes, slowing down, sometimes even stopping, to examine every object that seemed at first glance to be out of place. The only sounds were those of the insects, the wind sweeping the grass, and the noises of the horses: their hooves against the earth, the sweep of their heavy bodies through the tall grass, their snorting and blowing.

"Pudge."

All eyes turned toward the deputy, George, who had dismounted beside a flat, elongated boulder about halfway across the valley floor toward the highway.

"Everybody hold up right where you're at," shouted Pudge. Then he rode over to join George at the boulder.

"You got something, George?"

"Could be."

George was looking at a long, slender, dark object lying on top of the gray boulder. Pudge rode over closer to the rock and dismounted.

"That looks like one of them steel arrows," he said. "Like the one in the cabin wall."

"Yes sir," said George. "And that's not all. That sure looks like blood on it to me."

Pudge pulled a handkerchief out of his pocket and carefully picked up the arrow, wrapped in the handkerchief. He handed it to George.

"Looks like it, George," he said. "Here. Take this on into the lab and let's find out for sure."

Will McCarty had sidled over close enough to the boulder to spy on what was going on between the sheriff and his deputy, and when he saw his missing arrow and heard about the blood, his face went ashen. He kicked his horse in the sides and lashed at it with the reins, racing through the tall grass straight for the highway.

"Hey," shouted Pudge. "McCarty. Come back here."

Jack Wilder was the rider to the sheriff's immediate left and the one most likely to be able to intercept McCarty. Pudge and George were both on foot, and Hacker was closest to McCarty but showed no inclination to give chase. Jack took the situation in quickly and recalled the sheriff's earlier admonition about chasing criminals.

"Oh, hell," he said. Then he kicked the Appaloosa and headed him at an angle calculated to cut McCarty off before he reached the highway. Jack hadn't ridden hard like that for years, and he found that he liked the exhilaration. The Appaloosa moved through the tall grass with great leaping strides. McCarty wasn't managing his mount nearly as well as was Jack, but McCarty was making a beeline for the highway. Jack had a longer angle to ride. He was gaining on McCarty, but as he passed the boulder where Pudge and George were just mounting up, he realized that McCarty would make it to the highway well ahead of him. He reached for the coiled lariat that slapped at his right thigh, took the coils in his left hand and paid out a wide loop with his right. Swinging the loop over his head and riding hard, he tried to close the gap between himself and McCarty a little more. Then he released the main line, sending the wide loop out over McCarty's head. At just the right moment, Jack stopped the Appaloosa and took a few quick dallies around the saddle horn. McCarty suddenly felt himself jerked backward out of the saddle. The tall grass cushioned his fall to the ground somewhat, but he was still dazed by the shock long enough for Pudge and George to have mounted up and ridden over to where he lay. Pudge looked down at the stunned McCarty.

"George," he said, "you might as well take Mr. McCarty along with you when you head back for the office. Do you need any help?"

"No sir, I think I can handle it."

As George was getting McCarty to his feet and headed back toward the fenceline that ran along the ranch road, Monte Clark rode up to Jackson Wilder.

"Hey," he said, "where'd you learn that?"

"Uh, roping goats in Oklahoma," said Jack.

As Jackson busied himself recoiling the lariat, Pudge rode over beside Clark.

"Boy," he said, "don't you know anything? Jack Wilder was a rodeo champion before he started writing books. Course, that was while you were still in diapers."

George took the telltale arrow and its owner away in the sheriff's car, and Pudge Evans led the rest of the search party on across the valley floor to finish their sweep. It was largely a matter of just going through the motions, however, and nothing more of any interest was discovered. The riders came out on the highway and rode single file down the ditch beside the highway until they came to the ranch road, the long driveway, leading on back to the lodge. By that circuitous route, they made their way back. Monte Clark took charge of the horses, and Dack Hunter announced that the bar was open inside the lodge. Pudge went to the bar for a large lemonade, but the writers who had joined

the search headed for their cabins to get show-
ers. Sourdough just sort of faded away.

But it takes more than a shower to wash away
the effects of a ride on a hot summer day across
the dusty flat of an insect-ridden valley floor,
and soon the writers in their fresh clothes began
to emerge from their respective cabins and
make their entrances into The Old Corral. When
Jack and Maggie came in, Pudge Evans was no
longer in the room. They spotted Tom Brock
seated at a table with Myrna Keck and Donna
Doyle.

"Is this a private party?" asked Jack.

"Not hardly," said Myrna, with more than a
little exasperation apparent in her tone.

Brock stood up quickly and indicated the
empty chairs at the table.

"Sit down," he said. "I'll get the waitress over
here."

He waved wildly at the cowgirl behind the
bar, and she came rapidly to the rescue.

"What can I get for you folks?" she said
through a smile that would seem to have prevented articulation.

"I think I'll have a glass of that lemonade the
sheriff seems to like so much," said Jack. "How
about you, babe? Want a little glass of wine?"

"No," said Maggie, "I think I'll join you in the
lemonade."

Brock gestured toward the glasses in front of
himself and the two ladies in his company.

"We'll have another round here," he said.

The cowgirl trotted back to the bar.

"The sheriff go on back to town?" said Jack.

"No," said Brock. "I think he got a phone call in Dack's office. I don't know about you guys, but this thing is about to get the best of me."

Jackson reached over and slapped Brock on the shoulder.

"Don't let it get you down, buddy," he said. "You know, in spite of all the trouble, we've had a lot of fun up here. Isn't that right, Maggie?"

"Oh, yes. It's been wonderful," said Maggie. "Tom, don't blame yourself for whatever might have happened to Bob. That man, Krakes, was from New York. Whatever it was that happened here would probably have happened in New York if we'd never come here."

"I suppose you're right," said Brock.

The cowgirl came to the table and served the drinks, and about the same time, Pudge Evans came back into the room. Jack picked up his lemonade and followed Pudge to the bar.

"Well, Sheriff," he said, "what do you think?"

"Mr. Wilder," said the sheriff, "I wish you'd call me Pudge. All my friends do, and I'd like to count you among my friends. I haven't told you yet, but I'm a fan of yours. I think I've read all of your books. What's more, I was a fan of yours before you ever wrote a book—at least as far as I know. I watched you ride Double Trouble up at Cheyenne years ago."

"Woo-eee," said Jack. "That's taking me back some."

"About thirty years," said Pudge.

"Yeah, I wish you hadn't reminded me of that. As Maggie'd say, my hair was still black then."

"That was one hell of a ride, Mr. Wilder."

"That was one hell of a bull, Pudge, and the name's Jack."

"You were a damn good cowboy in those days," said Pudge.

"Yeah," said Jack. "Like you said, that was a long time ago."

"You still swing a pretty mean rope."

Jack laughed.

"Ah, well," he said, "hell, I knew I couldn't catch up with him. I had to do something."

Pudge took a long drink of lemonade. Then he reached in his pocket for a cigar. He wet the cigar in his mouth, struck a match on the bar and fired up.

"Jack," he said, "this is a real frustrating case. We've avoided saying it right out, but we both know that we're afraid that we might have a murder here."

Jackson shuddered at the word. Pudge was right. He had been doing his best to avoid even formulating the thought in his mind to that specific a point, and the verbalizing of it made him shiver.

"We can't arrest anyone for it, because we don't have a body," Pudge continued, "so I'm going to do what I can for the time being. I'm going to charge that New York private investigator with everything I can think of, and I'm going to charge McCarty with attempted murder on the basis of that arrow in the wall. By the way, I just talked to my deputy on the phone. He had the preliminary results of the lab tests on that other arrow. First of all, it is one of McCarty's. Presumably the one he says he tossed in the jeep with the bow. It's identical to the one shot in the wall. Second, it was human blood on the shaft, type AB negative."

"Oh God. That's Bob's type," said Jack.

"You sure?"

"Yeah. Yeah, I'm sure. My type is AB positive. Kind of rare. Bob used to brag to me that his blood was more rare than mine. AB negative is more rare than AB positive. It's his type all right."

"Well," said Pudge, "that don't necessarily mean it's his, but it's a hell of a coincidence if it ain't. I just thought you'd like to know the latest."

"Yeah. Thanks, Pudge. I appreciate that. Did, uh, did George talk to McCarty any?"

"Oh yeah. McCarty admits that the arrow is his. Said that it's the one he told us about. The one he dropped in the jeep. He had some others back in his cabin, and he says that he took them out and threw them in the big dumpster out back. He wanted to get rid of all the evidence that might link him to the arrow in the wall. I'll check the dumpster on my way out. He swears that he don't know how human blood got on that arrow or how it got out in the field. Says he ran off when he heard us talking about blood on an arrow because he panicked. He thought it looked too bad for him. He was making a run for the lodge, and then he thought that he'd grab a jeep and make for the airport or the state line or something."

"Do you believe him?"

"Hell, I don't know. Say, Dack Hunter tells me that his boys are putting on a little mini-rodeo for you folks tomorrow on your last day at the ranch. They got mini-everything these days. Anyhow they're planning to do that. You going to watch?"

"Sure. I'll watch it."

"You mind if I come out and join you?"

"Not at all, Pudge," said Jack. "I'd like that."

Pudge extended his right hand, and Jack took it in his.

"I'll see you then," said Pudge, and he waved at the room in general as he left to head back to town. Jack rejoined Maggie and the others at the table.

"How you doing, old girl?" he said.

"I thought you'd abandoned me."

"Oh, no. Not a chance. Now how could you think a thing like that? Hmm? Don't you know I love you—almost better than anything else in the world?"

"Almost?"

"Well, you know, there's Ajax. You know how I feel about Ajax."

Maggie slapped at Jack's forearm.

"Oh," she said, "you silly thing. You ought to love him better than me. You look like you're brothers."

"Come on now," said Jack. "That was uncalled for. That was really a mean thing to say to the man who loves you best."

"Except for Ajax."

"Well."

"Jack," Tom Brock interrupted.

"Yeah, Tom?"

"What did the sheriff have to say?"

"What, just now?"

"Yeah. What'd he have to say? Anything new?"

"Well, yeah, I guess so. He said he's going to charge Will with something for shooting that arrow. The arrow we found out in the valley today did have blood on it—and it was the same type as Bob's. That's about all."

"Oh, God," said Brock. He put his head in his hands, and Myrna Keck put an arm around his shoulder.

"Oh, yeah," said Jack. "He's going to charge that New York detective, too, with all kinds of stuff. I think that's all that was new."

"God," said Brock. "Bob's blood."

"No, now he didn't say that. We still don't know. All he said was that it was the same type."

"But it's bound to be Bob's," said Brock. "It couldn't be anyone else's."

Just then Jack felt a hard slap on his back.

"Hey, old man."

Jack winced at the voice and the unwelcome familiarity of Monte Clark.

"How you doing, kid?" he said. He couldn't tell whether or not his epithet had the same effect on its target as the other had had on him.

"You heard about our rodeo tomorrow?"

"Yeah. Yeah, we heard."

"You going to ride?"

Jackson turned in his chair and looked up into the face of Monte Clark incredulously.

"What?" he said.

"You're an old rodeo champ," said Clark. "You going to ride?"

"No. Hell, no, son," said Jack. "I quit rodeo before you were born."

"Why don't you ride and show us how it used to be done?"

"Excuse me, boy," said Jack. "I'm trying to talk to Mr. Brock here, all right? I'm not going to ride."

Jack turned away from Clark.

"Hey," said Clark, "I think you ought to show us young fellows how you used to do it in the old days."

"Monte."

The sharp voice came from behind Monte Clark, and the young cowboy turned to face Dack Hunter. Hunter gave Clark a stern look.

"Haven't you got anything you ought to be doing?" said Hunter.

"No," said Clark. "I got everything taken care of before I came in here."

"Monte, get out of here."

There was no mistaking Hunter's tone or intention. Clark's face burned red. He turned and left the room without another word.

"Mr. Wilder," said Hunter, "I apologize for Monte. I don't know what got into him. Maybe he had a bit too much to drink."

"Ah, that's all right, Hunter," said Jack. "That damn stuff will do real strange things to people. That's the reason I never touch it, myself. Is Monte riding in your little rodeo tomorrow?"

"Yes."

"Broncs or bulls?"

"Bulls. Monte's a bull rider."

"Well, good," said Jack. "I wish him a good draw. There's nothing like a tough bull to deflate an oversized ego. Maybe we'll get to watch him go down."

* * *

Pudge Evans trudged over to the big dumpster
behind the lodge and stood with his hands on his
hips. He stared at the big box as if it were a po-
tential foe. The lid was not quite shut, so Pudge
could tell that the dumpster was full. *Damn,* he
thought. *This could be an all-day job.* There was
bound to be garbage in there, too, as well as
trash. *Well, it's got to be done. And the hell of it is,
even if I find those damn steel arrows in there,
it's not going to help one damn bit. Not one way
or the other.* He lifted a heavy foot and stepped
on one of the steel extrusions on the side of the
dumpster, pulled himself up and threw back the
heavy lid releasing the stench of several days'
garbage. A cardboard box, crunched by the lid,
lay on top. Pudge gingerly picked it up and
tossed it to the ground. He heard the sound of a
car approaching the lodge by the ranch road,
and he dropped to the ground and walked over
to a point from which he could see around to the
front of the lodge. It was his own car returning.
He walked around to meet it.

George parked the sheriff's car in front of the
lodge just as Pudge appeared from around the
corner. The deputy crawled out of the car and
shut the door.

"George," said the sheriff, "go around back
and dig through that damn big trash can and see
if you can find Mr. Will McCarty's steel arrows
in there, would you?"

"Sure, Pudge," said George, and he headed
around the lodge. Pudge felt just a bit mean.
George was a good deputy and a pleasant and
agreeable young man. He never argued and

never complained. He, in other words, made it very easy for Pudge to shove off on him all the little unpleasant tasks that came their way, and Pudge took full advantage of the situation. *He's a good boy*, Pudge thought. He took a cigar out of his pocket, wet it, and struck a match against the side of his car. He was sending up great clouds of smoke when the front door of the lodge opened and Dack Hunter stepped out.

"Still around, Pudge," said Dack.

"Yeah. George is out back digging through your garbage."

"What's he looking for?"

"McCarty says that he tossed all his extra arrows in there. We just have to check it out."

"That's a big job and a nasty one," said Hunter. "I'll send a couple of the boys out there to give him a hand."

"Oh, thanks, Dack," said Pudge, feeling much better about having abandoned poor George to the filthy task. "He'll appreciate that."

The sheriff's cigar was just about gone when George came walking around the corner of the lodge holding by its strap a quiver of steel arrows. Pudge opened the car door and pulled the keys out of the ignition. He walked around to the trunk and opened it.

"Toss them in there," he said. "At least McCarty's telling us some truth."

The Appaloosa and the pinto were both loose in the corral rather than in their stalls. Jack Wilder caught them up and saddled them. Dack Hunter had offered to have a cowboy get the

horses ready for them when Jack had said that
he and Maggie wanted to go for a ride, but Jack
had said that he would like to catch and saddle
them up himself. So Dack Hunter had okayed it.
Jackson had gotten sick of the bar and the people in it, and he had asked Maggie if she'd like to
go for a ride. She had agreed immediately. Inside the bar there was a quiet tension, and most
of the others were just quietly getting a little
more drunk as the day passed. Pudge and his
deputy had gone back to town, and Tom Brock
was visibly—and more and more vocally—feeling sorry for himself. It bothered Jack that Bob
Drago was missing, maybe murdered, and Tom
Brock could only feel sorry for himself. He had
to get out. The physical activity of catching and
saddling the two horses was a relief.

There were really only two ways to ride from
the lodge—three if the road to the highway was
counted. They didn't want to ride down in the
valley again, so they took to the mountain road.
They didn't talk much, just a little small talk, as
they rode up the mountain. The ride was
enough. The horses were well rested and well
fed and feeling frisky, and the air tasted better
the farther they got up the mountain. When they
reached Monte Clark's favorite spot, the spot at
which the excursion had stopped to rest before,
they got off and tied the horses to the rail. Jack
paced up and down the side of the rail fence and
looked out over the valley. Finally he stopped
and leaned on the top rail.

"You know," he said, "if Bob's been killed, his
body's got to be out there somewhere."

Maggie stepped up beside him and put her

arm around his shoulders. It was a terrible thought. There might be a body out there somewhere in that vast, seemingly endless valley that used to house the man they had known as Bob Drago. It wouldn't be Bob, she told herself. She didn't know what to say to Jack. She just stood there beside him with her arm around him.

"You know, you were right about something," said Jack. "I wouldn't admit it when you said it, but you were right."

"About what, Jack?"

"About Bob and me competing with each other. You know, I admired Bob. I admired the hell out of him. He was always just a little bit better than me, just a little ahead of me. That didn't bother me. It gave me something to shoot for, you know? That's a kind of competition. But I think that it was important to Bob that he was better than me. What bothered me was not that he was so damn good, but that he tried to rub it in sometimes. He'd look for ways to remind me that he was out ahead. That, uh, that kind of bothered me."

"He did do that. I noticed it," said Maggie.

"Do you know when Bob started to fall apart?"

"Well, not exactly, but it was after they moved to New York, and I guess he'd started drinking pretty bad, and then he and Sylvia were having problems."

"Yeah. Yeah, that's right, but do you realize that it was right after my books had begun to outsell his? That's when it was. I've been thinking this all through very carefully, and that's when it happened. Whatever has happened to Bob Drago—whatever has happened here—it's all because of that competition between me and him that was so important to him. That's the reason for all this—this—whatever it is."

When they rode back to the corral to unsaddle the horses, old Sourdough was there. He was sitting on a wooden crate leaning against the barn and chewing tobacco. He spat in the dirt.

"Howdy," he said.

"Hi, Sourdough," said Maggie as she dismounted.

"Hey, old timer," said Jack.

"You're Jack Wilder, ain't you?" said Sourdough.

"Yeah, that's right."

"Used to rodeo."

"Yeah," said Jack. "A long time ago."

"I remember. Now you're one of them writers."

"Well, that's right."

"Cowboy books?"

"I write western novels."

"At least you been a cowboy. Not like some of them others."

Sourdough spat again.

"That Drago fellow. He was a friend of yours?"

"Yeah," Jack sighed. "A good friend. A long time ago back in Oklahoma."

"That's too bad," said Sourdough.

Jack pulled the saddle off the Appaloosa and tossed it over the top rail of the corral fence. Sourdough stood up and moved toward the pinto.

"Let me give you a hand," he said, and he unsaddled the pinto with an ease which belied his aged appearance.

"I knew something bad was going to happen here," he said. "I told Mr. Hunter, too. I knew it."

Jack stopped what he was doing and walked over close to Sourdough.

"How?" he said. "How did you know?"

"I could tell."

"What are you talking about, old timer? Huh? What do you mean?"

"Sneaking around. Talking secrets. I could just tell."

"Who was sneaking around and talking secrets? What did you see?"

"Your friend. Drago. That's who. I knew something bad was coming."

"Sourdough. Hey."

Sourdough was still busy with the pinto, and Jack grabbed him by the shoulders and turned him around to look him in the eye.

"Hey," he said. "Who was Bob talking to? Who did you see him with?"

Jack heard footsteps approaching from behind, and he looked over his shoulder to see Monte Clark ambling up.

"I'll put them horses up for you," said Monte. "Have a good ride?"

"Yes, we did," said Maggie.

"Well," said Sourdough, "I got to be getting along."

Jack looked after Sourdough for a moment, wanting to follow him and pursue the conversation further, but he thought better of it. Obviously, the old man had not wanted to be seen or overheard in their discussion. Well, he would find him later. Monte led the two horses to the corral, and Jack stepped over to Maggie's side.

"Maggie," he said quietly, "that old cook knows something."

Chapter Seven

"EXCUSE ME, Mr. Wilder."

Jackson Wilder looked up from his breakfast to see Dack Hunter standing across the table from him.

"Good morning," said Jack.

"Good morning," said Hunter. Then he nodded politely toward Maggie, seated at Jack's right. "Mrs. Wilder. Could I have a word with you?"

"Sure," said Jack. "Sit down."

Hunter pulled out a chair and sat at Jack's left. He motioned to the cowgirl to bring him a refill for his coffee cup, which he had carried with him.

"Mr. Wilder, a lot of folks around here, rodeo fans, remember you from your rodeo days. You still have some fans from those days."

Jack chuckled.

"I'd think that they'd be thinning out some by now," he said.

"Well, I don't know about that, but they're still around. I wonder if I might prevail upon you to lead the grand entry. You and Mrs. Wilder. I'd have those two horses you two've been riding all saddled up and ready to go. All you'd have to do is to climb on them and ride around the arena. We'll have an announcer, and, of course, he'll announce your names. Matter of fact, to be perfectly honest with you, it was his idea. When he heard that you were here, he suggested that I ask you."

"That right?" said Jack. "Who's your announcer?"

"Ford Cowan."

"Really? He's top-notch. One of the best. Is he here?"

"No, he's not here yet. Well, he just lives in Sheridan. He'll be coming out this evening for the rodeo."

"Well, yeah. I think we could do that. You want to do that, honey? Ride in the grand entry?"

"I'd like to," said Maggie. "It'll be fun."

"Yeah," said Jack. "We'll do it. You tell Cowan that we'll do it. And thanks for the offer. I'm, uh, I'm honored."

"Great," said Hunter, getting up from his chair. "Great. I'll tell Ford that you two will lead the grand entry. We'll all be looking forward to it. Thanks, Mr. Wilder. Mrs. Wilder, thanks."

Hunter took Jack's right hand and pumped it vigorously a few times, then made his exit.

"How about that?" said Jack.

"I think that's nice," said Maggie.

"So I'm still a hotshot rodeo star. Ha."

"That's pretty good. People do remember you, Jack."

"Yeah, well, I have to admit it's fun."

"Well, I'm ready to go," said Maggie. "I want to get back to the cabin and brush my teeth. And I want to change these shoes. Oh, and now that we're going to ride in the grand entry, I want to figure out what to wear. Are you ready?"

"Yeah, let's go."

They were outside walking toward the cabin when Jack spotted Sourdough. The old man had just stepped out of the barn, and it appeared to Jack that when Sourdough saw him, he had stepped back inside hurriedly.

"Hey," he said to Maggie, "you go on. I'll catch up to you in a little bit."

"What is it?" said Maggie.

"I just saw old Sourdough duck into the barn —like he's avoiding me. I want to talk to him. Okay?"

"Okay. I'll be in the cabin."

Jack trotted to the barn. The door through which Sourdough had emerged, then disappeared again, was closed. Jack climbed over the corral fence and walked over to the barn door. He pushed the door, and it opened slowly with a loud creak. It was dark inside the barn. Jack stepped into the doorway and tried to look around the inside, but he couldn't see.

"Hey, Sourdough."

There was no answer.

"Sourdough, I saw you come in here. I know you're here."

"What do you want?"

"I want to talk to you."

Sourdough was suddenly standing right before Jack's face. Jack jumped slightly.

"What do you want?" the old man said again.

"I just want to talk to you, buddy," said Jack. "You said that you had seen Bob Drago talking to someone. Said they acted kind of suspicious. Secretive."

"I seen them," said Sourdough. "Heard them, too."

"Who was Bob talking to?"

"Get on out of here," said Sourdough. "Someone might've seen you come in here. Get on out."

"Just tell me who you saw Bob with. Okay?"

"Come back here after dark. After the rodeo. Come back then and I'll tell you—maybe."

Sourdough vanished back into the darkness of the interior of the barn as suddenly as he had appeared.

"Sourdough. Hey. Hey, come here."

There was no answer. Jack decided that if the old cook didn't want to talk to him, there would be no point in trying to search for him in the darkness.

"Damn," he said, and he stepped back out into the light of day and shut the barn door. He would come back after the rodeo. Maybe he'd learn something then from the old man. As he walked back toward the cabin to rejoin his wife, Jack wondered who had been talking secretively to Bob Drago. What secrets could they have had? Everyone at the ranch seemed to have more or less ostracized Drago because of his obnoxious behavior, but if Sourdough was right, he had been intimate with someone. This could be a key to the whole mystery. He wondered if he should call Pudge or just wait to tell him when he showed up for the rodeo. Or should he not tell him at all until he had talked further with old Sourdough? Maybe what Sourdough had to say was nothing worth bothering about. The old man acted a bit of the fool after all. He'd see what Maggie thought about this.

Sourdough reached into his pocket for his tobacco plug. He didn't need light to pull out his jackknife and cut the plug, no more than he needed light to find his way around in the barn. He put the fresh chew in his mouth.

"Sourdough."

"Who's that?" said the old man.

"You've been talking to Jack Wilder."

"Who's there?"

"What have you been telling Wilder, old man?"

"I ain't told him nothing," said Sourdough. "What could I tell him? I ain't said nothing. Say, I know who you are."

"That's too bad, Sourdough. You shouldn't have said that."

"Huh? What do you mean?"

"You crazy old man. You'd have been smart to keep your mouth shut."

"What? Wait a minute. I didn't say nothing. I didn't talk to Wilder. He wanted to talk to me, but I didn't talk to him."

"But now you know who I am."

"No. No, I don't. I lied. I don't know you. Leave me alone."

"All right, Sourdough. I'll leave you alone. I'll leave you absolutely alone in just a few minutes."

The crowd was already gathering at the rodeo arena, which lay back behind the lodge, when the sheriff's car pulled up in front of the cabin in which Jack and Maggie Wilder were staying. It was early evening and just a little unusually warm, the last day for Brock and his clients at the Hunter Ranch.

"Pudge is here," said Jack. "Are you ready?"

He was anxious, the excitement even of a "mini-rodeo" having reached something deep inside him.

"Yes, I'm ready," said Maggie.

"Good. Let's go then."

Jack opened the door. Pudge had stepped out of the car, leaving its engine running.

"You folks ready to go?" asked the sheriff.

"Yeah," said Jack. "Yeah, Maggie will be right out, Pudge. How you doing this fine day, old buddy?"

"Not too bad. Thought I'd drive us over there. Air conditioning."

"Oh, sounds great. Hey, babe, you coming?"

"Yes, Jack," said Maggie from inside the cabin. "I'm just changing my shoes."

"Oh, I see. Okay. Well, Pudge, it'll be just a minute, I guess."

"No hurry."

"In a way, there is. You see, Maggie and I,

we've been asked to ride in the grand entry, so we really need to get on down there."

"That's great," said Pudge. "Dack's idea?"

"No. No, it wasn't. He asked us to do it, but he said that it was Ford Cowan who put the thought in his head."

"Yeah. That makes more sense. Dack don't know much. He's a good enough fellow, but he wouldn't have a damn thing if his daddy hadn't left it to him."

"Anyhow, that's all we're going to do, so if you can save us a spot, we'll come on up and sit with you as soon as we're done."

Maggie came to the door.

"Well," she said, "what are we waiting for?"

Jack looked at Pudge and shrugged his shoulders. They got into the sheriff's car, feeling the mild shock of the air conditioning, and Pudge drove them down to the arena. Some locals had joined the ranch guests to make a respectable crowd.

"Looks like we're just about on time here," said Pudge. "I see some space right over yonder on the front row."

"Okay, buddy," said Jack. "We'll join you there in just a bit."

Both the Appaloosa and the pinto knew what a grand entry was. They had been there before. They had known just as soon as they had been saddled and bridled in the special fancy rigs, and they pranced in anticipation. Jack and Maggie had dressed in their best western garb, too. Of course, they had not known they would be riding in the grand entry of a "mini-rodeo," but they had, after all, packed for a few days at a dude ranch. Maggie had brought some nice riding clothes with her, and Jack's only suit was one with a western cut. When they climbed into the saddles, they looked right at home. Monte Clark rode up close to Jack.

"I see you decided to ride after all," he said, a silly smirk on his face.

"Just enough to make you look good, sonny boy," said Jack.

Monte rode on back and took his place in line. Jack and Maggie had the lead, and Dack Hunter rode right behind them, carrying the flag.

"Ladies and gentlemen," the voice of Ford Cowan came over the loudspeaker, "welcome to the Hunter Dude Ranch mini-rodeo. That's what they told me to call it—mini-rodeo. I guess that means that it's not a big, full-scale rodeo, but let me tell you, folks, that don't mean that you won't see some good rodeo here tonight. All the competing cowboys and cowgirls work right here on the Hunter Ranch. I've seen these boys and girls before, and they are good. I can guarantee you that they're going to give you a real good action packed show. The stock is good, too, and it's Hunter Ranch stock. And just to get us off to the right kind of start, we have a couple of very special guests riding at the head of the grand entry. I'm real happy to introduce to you, right down there in the arena at the head of the line, riding that fine Appaloosa, former champion bull rider Jack Wilder. Give him a big hand, ladies and gentlemen."

The crowd roared as Jack took off his Stetson and waved it, and the grand entry began to

parade around the arena. It felt good to Jack—
the Appaloosa prancing underneath him, the rodeo crowd roaring again.

"Jack's not riding bulls anymore," said Cowan,
"he's writing western novels, and if you haven't
read them, I recommend that you run right out
and buy yourself one. I've read all of them, myself. Jack's still riding, or writing, out of Oklahoma, and we're real glad to have him up here
in Wyoming with us for this event. And right beside him, ladies and gentlemen, is his lovely
wife, Maggie. Maggie Wilder, all you real rodeo
fans will remember, was one of the top barrel
racers in rodeo at one time. So we have leading
our grand entry down there two former rodeo
champions. Jack and Maggie Wilder."

There was more applause and there were
more cheers. Maggie waved at the crowd, and
she, too, felt the old thrill return. It seemed to
the Wilders that the grand entry was over in just
a minute but when the last rider had cleared the
arena, they were called back out by Ford Cowan.
They turned their horses back toward the arena,
and Jack called out to Dack Hunter.

"You want to ride out with us and pick these
horses up, Dack?" he said.

"Sure."

Hunter followed Jack and Maggie back out
into the arena, but he kept a respectable distance. After all, it was their bow. They rode to
the center and waved their hats, prancing their
mounts around in a small circle in order to acknowledge the entire crowd. Then Jack put his
Stetson back on.

"Follow me, babe," he said, and he rode di-

rectly to the spot on the front row where Pudge
Evans waited with seats saved beside him. Jack
reached up and grabbed the steel rail that bor-
dered the grandstand. He pulled himself up and
out of the saddle and climbed over to the seats.
Then he reached down to help Maggie do the
same. Dack Hunter picked up the abandoned
horses and rode with them out of the arena.

"The pickup man there is Dack Hunter, folks,"
said Ford Cowan over the loudspeaker, "owner
of the Hunter Ranch."

The crowd applauded for Hunter as Jack and
Maggie took their seats beside Pudge.

"Oh, that was fun," said Maggie. "It's been a
long time."

"Yeah," said Jack. "Yeah, that was all right. Before he gets out of here, I want to meet Cowan
and thank him for remembering us like this."

"Yes," said Maggie, "we should do that."

"You two looked real sharp out there," said
Pudge. He was puffed up. He felt like he had
shared in the limelight, especially when they
had climbed over the rail to sit beside him.

Barrel racing was the first event, and Maggie
got excited and yelled for the cowgirls. The third
rider was the cowgirl from behind the bar in
The Old Corral. She was the only one that Maggie sort of knew, so she was glad when the waitress's time proved to be the best. The second
event was calf roping. Jack watched with a
trained and critical eye.

"These boys are pretty good," he remarked to
Pudge.

An exhibition of team roping came next.
There was no competition in that event, the

Hunter Ranch not having put together enough roping teams from its crew, but the exhibition was a good one. Then the real excitement began. The bucking events were all that remained. Four cowboys attempted to ride bareback. Three were thrown, one rather spectacularly. Ford Cowan said that he did a "one and a half" off that horse's back. The cowboy got up and walked away unhurt. One cowboy made the full eight seconds and was expertly removed from the bucking bronc's back by the pickup men.

"The next event is the saddle-bronc riding, folks," announced Cowan, "and right now down in chute number two, the first rider is getting himself ready. That's Monte Clark, and he's on yo-yo."

Jack looked at Pudge.

"I thought Clark was a bull rider," he said.

"So did I," said Pudge.

Down in the chute yo-yo banged against the steel gate. Monte Clark grabbed the top rail with his free hand.

"Yo-yo is bad in the chute," said Cowan. "Monte Clark has got his work cut out for him today. Now it looks like he's got yo-yo settled down. He's ready to go. He's nodding his head. The gate's open, and here we go. He spurred him out good. Look at that ride. Good spurring action. Yo-yo's doing his job, too. There's the buzzer. We have a qualifying ride, and it was a good one. Clark's just looking for a way off now."

Just then yo-yo made a leaping buck, and Monte Clark, ready for it, vaulted out of the saddle, landing on his feet on the arena floor. He swept the hat off his head and waved it at the crowd, and Jack Wilder felt like for sure he, personally, received a haughty glance from Clark. The next cowboy up was thrown, and the last three made qualifying rides, but Monte Clark received the highest score. Then Ford Cowan announced the bull riding.

The first bull out of the chute made some feeble hops for eight seconds, and the embarrassed cowboy received a score of sixty-nine for his ride. The second was ready to go.

"We don't know what this bull's going to do after that first turn," said Cowan. "Nobody's ever made it past there with him. Let's see what this cowboy does."

The gate was jerked open, and the bull lunged out into the arena. He made a fast turn, his powerful haunches jerking around after the front of his body. The cowboy dropped to the ground almost inside the chute. The clown, or bullfighter, was right there on the spot to attract the bull's attention away from the fallen cowboy.

"Back down in chute number one, ladies and gentlemen," said Cowan, "we have Monte Clark, and he's riding Billy the Kid. Monte just gave us a fine ride in the saddle-bronc event, folks, and he's right back to see if he can handle this bull. This boy's a real competitor."

In the chute Monte pounded and strapped down his gloved left hand. He pulled on the rigging and tightened and retightened it until he felt sure it was right. Then he slapped himself in the face with his free right hand several times. Finally he nodded his head in quick little jerks, and the gate was swung wide. Billy the Kid

bolted. He shot straight up in the air. The clown
ran around the action, keeping close. Billy the
Kid made three leaping bucks toward the center
of the arena. He spun. He bucked. Monte Clark,
like a rag doll, snapped back and forth on his
back. Just below where the Wilders sat with
Pudge Evans, the massive beast made a quick
twist and followed it with a high, hard buck.
Monte went off to his right, his hand caught in
the rigging. The bull gave his body a couple of
brutal bangs against its broad side before the
clown managed to get hold of the rigging in an
attempt to free Monte. Billy the Kid tossed them
both around. Then the clown finally pulled Monte's hand loose and both men fell to the ground
there below the sharp hooves.

In an instant Jackson Wilder had analyzed the
situation and vaulted over the railing to land di-
rectly in front of the raging bull.

"Jack," shouted Maggie.

The bull turned on Jack, allowing the clown to
drag Monte Clark to safety. As Monte climbed
the fence and the clown was turning back to his
job, the bull lowered its head menacingly, and
Jack turned and sat on the broad expanse of
hard forehead, grabbing a horn in each hand.
The angry animal flung Jack through the air
with an easy toss of its head. Jack landed hard
and rolled in the dirt, came to his feet running
and climbed the fence. Billy the Kid was by this
time chasing the clown. Jack walked around the
stands to happy applause until he came back to
his seat, and then he sat back down beside his
wife.

"Oh, Jack, you fool," said Maggie. "You were marvelous."

"How about that, ladies and gentlemen?" Cowan roared over the loudspeakers. "How about that for excitement? That was Jack Wilder, ladies and gentlemen. Jack Wilder. Still a champion."

The crowd roared its approval, and Jack stood up and waved. Then he sat back down.

"That was quick thinking," said Pudge. "You just might have saved that boy's life."

"Oh, I don't know," said Jack. "I didn't think at all. If I had, I'd have just sat still. You know, I think that little jerk was showing off for me. I must have the same mentality."

"What do you mean, Jack?" asked Maggie.

"I mean that I was probably just showing off back at him. Hell of a note."

The crowd continued to show its appreciation with applause. Jack felt a little embarrassed, especially since his quick analysis of his own motivation. He also felt a little of the old sensation of the thrill of applause following a good ride. But that had been a long time ago, and, he realized, he was also in a certain amount of pain. Safe behind a gate and feeling his own pain, Monte Clark looked across the arena at Jack, the puzzlement plain on his face.

"Oh," said Jack, stretching his back and wincing with the pain, "I'm way too old for this."

Jack and Pudge headed for the barn in the darkness. Jack limped slightly from his show-off escapade at the mini-rodeo and wondered if the showing off or the possible saving of Monte

Clark had been worth the aches and pains. As they got closer to the barn, Pudge stopped and put a hand on Jack's shoulder.

"I'll wait for you here," he said. "If Sourdough was reluctant to talk to you, he may really clam up if he sees me along. If you need me, or if you find out that he's willing to talk with me around, just give a holler. I'll be right here."

"Okay," said Jack. He walked alone on over to the corral, where he thought briefly about climbing the fence. His aches told him that was not a good idea. He opened the gate, went through and closed it again behind himself. Then he went to the barn door. It was standing open, and the interior was even darker than before. Jack stepped inside.

"Hello?" he called tentatively.

There was no answer from within, and Jack felt like he was giving a repeat performance of an absurdist play.

"Hey," he said. "It's Jack Wilder. Anybody here?"

The darkness and the quiet inside the barn were almost palpable.

"Hey, Sourdough. Are you in here? Dammit."

Jack turned toward where he had left Pudge Evans and called out to the sheriff.

"Hey, Pudge," he said. "Come on over."

Pudge crunched through the darkness to the corral gate where Jack was waiting for him.

"If he's in there, he won't answer me," said Jack.

"You don't suppose he saw me coming with you?" asked Pudge.

"Ah, I don't know. In this dark, I doubt it. Dammit. He knows something, Pudge. I'm sure of it. He knows something about Bob Drago and somebody, but I think he's scared. He's scared of someone. Dammit, he said he'd be here tonight. I figured he'd tell me."

"Let's take a look inside," said Pudge.

"You can't see a damn thing in there," said Jack.

"This will help."

Pudge pulled a flashlight loose from his belt and snapped it on. Then he went through the gate and across the corral to the barn door. He shined the light around from the doorway, and, seeing nothing unusual from there, went inside. Jack followed, and they examined the inside of the barn closely.

"Well," said Pudge, "there's nothing here that shouldn't be, and there's nobody here, whether they should be or not."

"There's sure no sign of Sourdough," said Jack.

"Jack, you want my suggestion?"

"What's that?"

"This is your last night at the ranch. You're going back to Oklahoma in the morning, right?"

"That's right."

"Everybody's gathered for the last time in The Old Corral up at the lodge. Try to put all this out of your mind. I know it ain't easy, but try. Let's go on over to the lodge and join the others. I'll find Sourdough and take him in for questioning. I'll ask around some tonight, and if I don't find him, I'll be back out here first thing in the morning. You've done all you can do. Leave it to me from here on. Okay?"

"Well," said Jack, "that's probably pretty good advice. Anyhow, it's about all I can do. Let's go."

As Pudge had said, there was one last gathering in The Old Corral. Dack Hunter had brought in a local singer of cowboy songs for entertainment. The man was crooning "Empty Saddles in the Old Corral." Tom Brock began to worry about paying the bill. He could well afford to pay it, yet he worried. The two romance writers sat up close to the bandstand and gazed longingly at the cowboy singer, who, as Maggie remarked to Jack, was quite good. Jack and Maggie sat with Tom Brock and his secretary, Myrna, and after a while, Pudge Evans paid them a surprise visit and joined them at their table with a giant lemonade. Jack had developed a liking for the tough-looking sheriff and was glad to have his company. To poor Tom Brock, Evans represented all that had gone wrong with his planned celebration. No one talked of the missing Robert Drago or of the surrounding mysteries. Jack was trying hard to take Pudge's advice. The night was still young to the serious drinkers when Pudge Evans excused himself.

"Some of us have to work in the morning," he said.

"Well," said Jack, "all I have to do in the morning is get up and catch a plane, but I think maybe I'll turn in, too. What do you say, sweet?"

"I am tired," said Maggie.

They said good night to the others and walked

out of the lodge with the sheriff. Jack and Pudge shook hands at the sheriff's car.

"Pudge," said Jack, "it's been a pleasure."

"Don't be a stranger, huh?" said Pudge.

"Well," said Maggie, "we don't get up to this part of the country very often, I'm afraid."

"You're both writers. Write me a letter now and then."

"Yeah, we'll do that," said Jack. "Listen. If you should find out anything more . . ."

"I'll let you know," said Pudge.

They said good-bye, and Pudge drove away. Jack and Maggie walked hand in hand back to their cabin. They spent an hour or so getting packed for the trip home—everything except what they would need in the morning. Jack set the alarm clock to get them up in plenty of time. No one else had the same flight time as they did, so the plan was for Monte Clark to drive them in again in the jeep; therefore, Jack wasn't looking forward to the ride. Maggie was first in bed. She turned on the lamp on her bedside table while Jack checked the door to be sure that it was locked, then turned off the overhead light. He crawled in bed, leaned over to reach across Maggie and turn off the lamp, and as he switched it off, bent to kiss her.

It was well past midnight when a noise outside awakened Maggie. She opened her eyes and lay still for a moment, trying to make sense out of what she was hearing. Finally she eased herself out of bed and felt around in the dark for her gown, which had been discarded shortly after Jack had turned off the lamp. She found it on the floor beside the bed and put it on. Then she went to the window and eased the curtain aside enough to allow her to peer cautiously outside. She saw a figure standing near the jeep that was parked at their door. In the dark it was not much more than a silhouette. Maggie went back to the bed and gave Jackson a shake. As he started to come out of his sleep and vocalize his puzzlement, Maggie shushed him.

"There's someone outside," she whispered.

"Huh? What's he doing?"

"Just standing there."

Jack was pulling on his jeans.

"Where?" he said.

"Right outside the door. Just beside the jeep."

Jack peeked out the curtain the way Maggie had done. The figure was still there. It shuffled around as if hesitating—trying to make up its mind. Jack went to the door and opened it. He was about to challenge the figure when it spoke up first, stepping forward.

"Mr. Wilder?"

"Monte?" said Jack. "Monte Clark? Is that you?"

"Yes, sir."

"What the hell are you doing here? You scared my wife half to death."

Jack knew as he said it that he was lying, but it seemed like an appropriate comment to make.

"I'm sorry, Mr. Wilder," said Clark, keeping his voice low. "I didn't know what to do. I saw someone."

"What are you talking about?"

"Just now. I was coming out of the lodge, and I saw someone sneaking around behind the cabins. The sheriff's already gone home. I thought about waking up Mr. Hunter, and then I thought about you. I couldn't make up my mind to go ahead and wake you up. When I came over here, I was hoping that you'd still be up."

"Where'd you see this guy?"

"Well," said Monte, pointing, "he came right out from behind that cabin, the one Mr. Drago was in, and then he ran over that way."

"How long ago?"

"Just a minute. I've only been here for a minute or so."

"Come on."

"Jack," said Maggie from the doorway.

"Just shut the door and lock it, babe," said Jack.

Jack led Monte to the rear of the cabin, staying close to the wall and in the shadows. They stood in silence at the back corner for a moment and watched. Jack caught a glimpse of movement down the row of cabins and touched Monte on the arm. He pointed. Monte looked and saw it too. He nodded to let Jack know. They moved in the shadows toward the skulking figure. Jack thought, *Here I go again. I should be calling Pudge, and that's just what he'll say later.* The figure suddenly emerged from the dark shadows and ran for the front of a cabin.

"Let's go," said Jack, and he led Monte quickly to the front of the cabin they had been hiding behind. Two cabins down the row, the dark figure moved to the front door. Jack ran, with Monte right on his heels. The figure knocked at the door and it opened for him. There was only a faint light from inside the cabin.

"That's Miss Keck's cabin," said Monte.

The door shut just before Jack reached it, and he banged on it with his fist.

"Open up," he shouted.

Whoever had shut the door had not locked it; in fact, in his apparent haste, had not even shut it well. It opened to Jack's pounding. There was a shriek, and Myrna Keck, standing naked beside the bed, grabbed at the bedspread to try to cover herself. The male figure sitting on the side of the bed turned to face the intrusion.

"God damn it, Jack. Do you have to ruin everything?"

Jack stood stupidly in the doorway staring at Tom Brock and his red-faced secretary. He took hold of the door handle to pull the door shut behind himself as he backed away.

"Uh, excuse me," he said. "It's all a mistake."

He looked at Myrna Keck and nodded.

"Have fun," he said, "and, uh, lock the door, huh?"

He pulled the door shut and started to walk back to his own cabin. Monte Clark stepped along beside him.

"Well," said Jack, "that's about enough adventure for tonight, I think."

Back at his cabin, he tapped lightly on the door.

"Jack?" came Maggie's voice from inside.

"Yeah. It's me."

Maggie quickly unlocked the door and opened it. Jack stepped inside.

"Are you all right?"

"Yeah," he said, heading for the bathroom. "I've got to wash my feet."

"Well, what was it?"

"False alarm," he said. "Nothing at all."

He dropped his jeans to the floor, turned on the water and stepped into the tub.

Monte Clark stood alone in the darkness. He was embarrassed—more than that—he was humiliated. First of all, he had gotten slightly drunk the other day, and he had wised off at Jack Wilder in The Old Corral. Jack Wilder was a highly respected man, and Monte had undoubtedly made a fool of himself. Then to make it worse, he had been chastised for it by his boss in front of everybody in the place. Still smarting from that episode, he had tried his best to show off, to be cocky, in front of Wilder at the rodeo, and that had backfired on him. He had taken a bad fall from a bull and had been rescued by Wilder from what might have been a very bad stomping. And now this thing. He had really made a fool of himself. He was not looking forward to having to drive the Wilders to the airport in the morning.

Monte had had a few drinks at The Old Corral just before he had seen the shadowy figure that had turned out to be Tom Brock, and that, along with the apprehension and then the final humiliation, made him feel just a bit woozy. He wanted some water to splash on his face. Maybe even a drink of water. He staggered toward the corral, where a watering trough stood just inside the gate. Even in his state, Monte didn't bother with opening the gate. He climbed over and dropped to the ground on the inside of the corral. He lurched toward the trough and plunged his face into the water. The trough was full almost up to the top. Water ran over the edge as Monte splashed in it. Then he felt something solid from underneath the water brush against his face. Something solid yet soft. He jerked his face out of the water. It took a few seconds for him to wipe the water from his eyes and focus his vision on the trough, then to see in the darkness through the water.

"Oh, my God," he said. "Oh, God. Jesus."

There laid out in the trough as if it were a coffin and floating just below the surface of the water, staring through blank watery eyes and looking slightly bloated, was the body of old Sourdough. Monte wanted to turn and run, but instead he sank to his knees and puked there beside the trough.

It was almost two o'clock in the morning when Pudge Evans showed up at the ranch again. He had George with him and, this time, the county coroner. Photographs were taken, and Sourdough was fished out of the trough. Jack Wilder and Monte Clark were interviewed. No information came forth other than the body itself. The coroner make a quick and hasty examination that indicated that Sourdough had been strangled before he had been placed in the trough, but he said that he would not be absolutely sure until he had made a thorough examination. The coroner took the body away, and Pudge Evans stood leaning on the corral fence. Jack Wilder walked over to stand beside him.

"Well," said Pudge, "now we know why Sourdough didn't keep his appointment with you."

"I guess we do," said Jack. "He'd still be alive if I'd left him alone."

"Bull," said Pudge.

Jack was surprised at the sudden harshness of the sheriff's language.

"Sourdough's dead because he saw something that somebody didn't want him to see," the sheriff continued, "and even then, he might still be alive if he had told you or me or somebody what he saw early enough for us to have prevented this. If it's anybody's fault besides the killer's, it's his own."

Jack stood still, not bothering to try to respond to Pudge's sudden tirade. The sheriff expelled a long and tired sigh.

"We've got a body now," he said. "It's not the one we were looking for. Not the one we were expecting to find, but we've got one. It's a murder case now for sure."

"Pudge," said Jack, "should I stick around? I could change my flight out of here to some other time."

"No. You go on home."

"I just feel like I'm walking out in the middle of something unfinished. I don't feel right about it."

"There's nothing else you can do, Jack. Just go on home."

Chapter Eight

"CHECK THE BATHROOM," said Maggie. "Did you get your toothbrush?"

"Yes. I got it. I'm all packed."

"What about your razor?"

"All right. All right. Look. I'm in the bathroom. I'm checking the bathroom all over again. There's nothing left in here. Okay?"

"Okay. I'd better check all these drawers again just to make sure. I'd hate to leave something."

"I don't know what we brought that we could leave that we'd miss very much when we get back home," said Jackson.

"Your Grandpa Wilder's shaving stuff," said Maggie. "You'd miss that."

"Well, it's all packed."

"How about the closet?" said Maggie.

"I'm looking in the closet right this very minute just to satisfy you, my love. There's nothing in the closet but some empty hangers. Is it all right to leave them here?"

Maggie stood in the center of the room and looked around, her hands on her hips.

"Well," she said, "I guess we're ready."

Jackson opened the front door and looked out.

"Well, that's good," he said, "because here comes our ride right now."

He turned to pick up the two heaviest suitcases and headed outside with them to meet the jeep.

"Good morning, Mr. Wilder," said Monte as he shut down the jeep's engine. "Are you folks about ready?"

Well, thought Jack, *I'm carrying the damn suitcases out. What does it look like to you?*

"Yeah," he said.

Maggie came out with the two smaller bags.

"Let me get those for you," said Monte.

He took the two bags from her and tossed them in the back of the jeep. Jack had heaved one bag in already, and Monte reached for the second heavy one. Jack stepped back and watched, a little curious.

"What about the keys?" said Maggie "I have the jeep key here and the key to the cabin. What do you want me to do with them?"

"Oh, you could have left them inside, but I'll take them," said Monte.

Jack climbed into the jeep's back seat, and Monte helped Maggie into the front.

"Thank you," she said.

Monte trotted around the jeep and hopped behind the wheel. Jack couldn't help but wonder what had the young cowboy in such a good mood. The two of them had, after all, sort of made fools of themselves the night before, and before that Monte Clark had not exactly given the impression that he was an admirer of Jackson Wilder. And then there was the ghastly discovery that Monte had made.

Maybe he's just glad to be getting rid of me, he thought.

The ride into Sheridan seemed longer to Jack than it should have. Monte Clark alternately whistled the tunes to cowboy songs or made small talk to Maggie. Jack settled into the back seat and tried to let the wind drown out all other sounds. He thought about getting back home. There was an unfinished novel waiting for him there. He wondered how Ajax was doing. And then there was that intruder into his house. Sherman had said that everything seemed to be okay. Still, it would be reassuring to get home and look things over for himself. A week away from home was enough. It would feel good to be back.

At the airport Monte Clark pulled the jeep up to the curb in front of the terminal. He shut off the engine and set the parking brake. Jumping out, he ran around to the back of the jeep and hauled out the bags, the heavy ones first. By the time Jackson had climbed out of the back seat, Monte had all four bags lined up on the sidewalk.

"Thank you, Monte," said Maggie. "We can handle it from here."

"All right," said Monte. "It's been a real pleasure, ma'am."

Jack picked up the two heavy bags and started to turn to go into the terminal.

"Mr. Wilder," said Monte.

Jack looked at the cowboy.

"Yeah?"

Monte took two quick steps back to the jeep and reached under the front seat. He pulled out a paper bag.

"Mr. Wilder," he said, reaching into the bag and drawing out a new, hardcover copy of *Six-gun Range*, "would you sign this for me? It'll just take a minute. I bought it. And I read it. It's real good."

Jack set down the bags and took the book from Monte. He looked at it, then looked at Monte. He reached into his shirt pocket for a pen.

"Sure," he said.

He wrote in the book, reread what he had written, snapped the book shut and handed it back to Monte. He touched the brim of his hat.

"Take it easy, hot shot," he said, and he picked up the bags and went into the terminal followed by Maggie.

"Good-bye, Monte," Maggie called over her shoulder.

Monte Clark watched the Wilders leave his sight, then opened the book and read what Jackson had written there.

"To my friend, Monte Clark," it said, "a pretty good cowboy. Jackson Wilder."

"By God," said Monte, his chest swelling with pride and a broad smile spreading across his face. "By God."

At the airport in Tulsa, Jack and Maggie retrieved their luggage with only a slightly irritating wait, then made their way out to the long-term parking lot. Jack put down one of the heavy bags in order to use both arms to heave the other one over the side of the pickup.

"Dammit," he said.

"What is it, Jack?"

"The spare tire's gone," he said. "Someone took our spare. Dammit."

"Jack," said Maggie, "it's at home. Don't you

remember? You took it out before we left because the pickup was going to be sitting here unwatched all this time. It's at home."

"Is it?"

"Yes. It is."

"Did I do that?"

"Yes, you did."

"Well, that was pretty good thinking, wasn't it?"

"Yes, it was."

"You see, there's no spare here. Right? Now if I hadn't had the foresight to take it out before we left home, that would mean that it had been stolen. I just saved us the price of a new tire."

Jackson tossed the other three bags into the back of the pickup, walked to the passenger-side door, reached through the broken window wing and opened the door for Maggie.

"Special door lock," he said.

"I wish you'd get that fixed," said Maggie as she climbed into the cab.

"Yeah, I really should."

The familiar roads home felt good to Jack, and he took their curves with a little too much speed for Maggie's comfort.

"I wish you'd slow down," she said. "These curves are dangerous."

"I've been driving these roads all my life," said Jack. "Trust me. Know them like the back of my hand."

"That's a real original line."

"Best I can do right now, babe. I've got to keep my mind on my driving."

"Jack, slow down."

"Well, I . . . Uh-oh."

Jack hit the brakes as he topped a rise and found there before him, moving along at no more than thirty miles an hour, an old DeSoto.

"I think I'd better slow down," he said. "Grandpa's out for a Sunday drive."

"That's a real good idea," said Maggie. "We're almost home, anyway."

"My thoughts exactly."

The Ozark foothills roads that wind through much of eastern Oklahoma are narrow and shoulderless, and Jack had to content himself with poking along behind the DeSoto while the heavy truck traffic roared along in the opposite lane and cars and trucks piled up behind him. At the turnoff to his house, a left-hand turn, Jack flipped on the turn signal, and, because he wasn't at all sure that it was working, stuck his left arm out the window for a hand signal, bringing the long line of traffic behind him to a standstill.

"I hope that blinker's working," he said. "I don't think people know what hand signals are anymore."

At the first break in the stream of oncoming traffic, Jack popped the clutch and wrestled the steering wheel to make his left turn across the two-lane highway and onto the rocky, unpaved road that led up the hill and into the woods. About a half mile up the road, Jack made a right onto another dirt road and brought the pickup to a stop after driving another two hundred or so yards. He was parked on the road beside his mailbox. He stepped out of the pickup and opened the box.

"No mail today, babe," he said.

"Maybe Sherman has been by and picked it up."

"Maybe."

He climbed back into the truck and eased it into his long driveway. From somewhere off in the wooded acres there came a long and loud bleat. Jack shouted out the window in response.

"Hey, old goat," he said.

He parked the pickup and walked over to where the fence ran past the small barn to keep Ajax from climbing on the house and on any vehicles that might be parked in the driveway. The goat came bounding through the tall weeds. It let out a happy bleat of greeting.

"Oh," said Maggie, "he's glad that we're back home."

"Well, so am I," said Jack, reaching over the fence to grab Ajax by the horns and shake his head. "How are you, old whiskers? You doing all right? Damn, you've got the ticks."

"Where's Crackerjacks?" said Maggie.

"Ah, she's bashful. No. Worse. She's pregnant and she's ashamed. This old bastard ought to be ashamed, too. Aren't you ashamed of what you did to your sister? Huh? Aren't you ashamed?"

"Jack, he doesn't know what you're talking about. I'm going in the house, Jack."

"Yeah. All right. Say, would you bring me out a bucket of hot water?"

"How big?"

"Oh, it doesn't have to be big. A bucket, a pan, whatever. But hot."

Maggie headed for the front door while Jack unhooked the gate and slipped into the fenced area with Ajax. He squatted down beside the goat and patted its side.

"No wonder you're so damn bony," he said. "These old ticks are sucking all your blood out."

Ajax reached over and got the brim of Jack's Stetson with his teeth.

"Hey. Leave that alone. Give me that. Look at how tall these weeds are. If you're so damn hungry, eat some of these weeds down, will you? Leave my hat alone."

Ajax bleated a response, and Maggie came out of the house with a pan of steaming water. She handed it over the fence to Jack who put it on the ground beside him.

"Thanks, babe," he said. "Now, you just hold still, you old goat."

He pulled a fat, gray tick from between Ajax's ribs and dropped it into the hot water. The tick shriveled as the red blood began to color the water.

"There," he said. "That'll teach him."

Maggie turned her head.

"Euh," she said. "I'll be inside."

She turned and went back into the house as Jack tossed a second parasite to a boiling death.

"Take that, you bastard."

He stroked the goat's side feeling for another as Sherman Postoak turned into the driveway in his old pickup. Sherman drove on down to the house and shut off his engine.

"I'm over here, Sherm," Jack shouted.

"With the other goats?"

"Well, with at least one of them."

Sherman walked over to the fence.

"Boiling up a stew for supper?" he asked.

"Yeah," said Jack. "You're invited to stay."

He dropped a fat tick into the hot water.

"Die, damn you," he said.

"You know, Jack," said Sherman, "them ticks is just doing what God made them to do."

"Yeah? Well, so am I, Sherm. So am I."

"God made you to kill ticks? That your purpose in life? I wonder what your agent and your publisher and all your readers would think of that."

"Well, I don't know," said Jack, ending the life of another fat arachnid. "I know some critics, though, who would agree with it right now."

"You just get back?"

"Yeah."

Jack stood up and stretched. Ajax pulled his shirttail out, and Jack shoved his face away.

"Cut it out. That the thanks I get for cleaning you up? Go on. Go eat some grass. Yeah, we just got back. I haven't carried the suitcases in yet."

"Is that a hint?" said Sherman.

"No. No, I'll carry them in. You can watch me, and when I'm done, you can have a cup of coffee with me."

Jack slipped out of the fence and latched the gate behind himself. Ajax bleated at him.

"Come on," said Sherman, walking over to Jack's pickup. "I'll give you a hand with these things."

Sherman pulled one of the heavy bags out over the edge of the pickup.

"Damn, Jackson," he said. "What you got in here? Bricks?"

"No. Wyoming rocks. I'm starting a collection."

They carried the four suitcases into the house
and dropped them in the middle of the living-
room floor.

"Hey, babe," shouted Jack, "is there any coffee
on? Sherm's here."

Maggie came running into the room.

"Oh, hi, Sherman," she said. "Sherman, we
thank you so much for looking after things
while we were gone. I'll just go into the kitchen
and put on the coffee."

"Goksdi agwaduli," said Sherman.

Jackson patted his shirt pockets as if he were
looking for something in them, looked around
himself, then raised his hands in a gesture of
futility.

"I, uh, I don't have any," he said.

"Well, then," said Sherman, reaching into his
pocket for a pack of cigarettes, "we'll just have to
smoke mine, I guess."

Jack took a cigarette from Sherman and returned the pack.

"Let's go out on the porch," he said.

"No ashtrays?"

"No."

They stepped out onto the porch and lit their
cigarettes.

"Has everything been quiet out here since that
visitor you ran into?" said Jack.

"Ran into is right," said Sherman. "That's just
exactly what I did. Right over there. No, I
haven't seen him again. Him or anyone else.
Can't find anything missing or torn up or anything either."

"Well, you must have caught him before he got
around to whatever it was he was up to."

"I guess."

Jack took a last drag on his cigarette and threw the butt into the dirt.

"Well," said Sherman, "how was Wyoming?"

"Oh, it was all right. It was, uh, interesting."

"Different from Oklahoma, huh?"

"Yeah."

Jack stared off into the woods for a moment, the cool-appearing, shadowy, deep and inviting woods with their ticks and chiggers and other occasional prowlers.

"Sherman," he said, coming out of his brief reverie, "you remember a friend of mine who used to come around and visit us now and then with his wife? They lived in Oklahoma City. Moved up to New York about seven years ago. Bob Drago. Bob and Sylvia."

"Yeah, I remember them. You see them up in Wyoming?"

"No. Not exactly. Bob and Sylvia are not married anymore. We didn't see Sylvia. She wasn't there. Bob was up there at the ranch, though. That is, he was up there when we arrived. He disappeared the first night."

"What do you mean? He left?"

"He disappeared. He just disappeared."

"Jack," said Sherman, "a man don't just disappear. Not unless he's a *tsgili* or something like that. He don't just disappear. Especially a white man. *Yoneg.* He don't just disappear. He goes away. He hides. Somebody takes him away. Something."

"Well, that's just it," said Jack. "Nobody knows."

"Someone knows."

The front door opened and Maggie stuck her head out.

"The coffee's made," she said. "Do you want it out here?"

"No," said Jack, "we'll come inside."

Sherman threw his cigarette stub away and they went in. Maggie poured the coffee, and the three of them sat around the kitchen table.

"I was just telling Sherm about Bob," said Jack.

"Oh, yes," said Maggie. "It's so strange. We never did find out what happened to him."

"Maybe he just left," said Sherman. "Maybe he didn't like the dude ranch."

"Well," said Jack, "we thought about that. He was pretty drunk. Pretty much out of it. The condition he was in, he might've done anything. But he left without packing. It looked like he left everything behind. And the night he disappeared, someone shot an arrow into his room. One of those steel things. We found his jeep—they gave each of us a jeep to drive around while we were there—we found his driven off down the side of a mountain. There was a compound bow with it. Then we found an arrow like the one in his room out in the field with some blood on it. His type."

"And Jack caught a man going through Bob's things one night," said Maggie. "The man pulled a gun on Jack and they had a fight."

"Yeah," said Jack. "He turned out to be a New York private eye. They've got him locked up along with another guy—one of the writers, one of Tom's clients, guy named McCarty. McCarty admitted shooting the arrow. Says that the bow and the arrows are his. But he says that's all he did."

"Yes," said Maggie, "and the detective worked for some businessmen in New York that Bob had swindled out of one hundred thousand dollars, and there were some other things, but the last night we were there, a man was murdered."

"It was the ranch cook," said Jack. "He had said that he was going to tell me something about Bob."

"It's like I said," said Sherman. "Somebody knows. Start over and tell me everything again."

Jack and Maggie went through the whole story again, this time recalling other details and filling them in, like the saddled horse running loose, Drago's obnoxious behavior, the way everyone seemed to feel about Drago, and Sylvia's plans to remarry. Sherman listened intently. When they had finished the tale, he sat quietly for a moment.

"It all sounds pretty fishy," he finally said. "It's kind of interesting you running into all that action up there in Wyoming and somebody breaking into your place down here at the same time."

"You mean you think there might be some connection?" said Jack. "Naw. No, I don't think so. I can't imagine what it could be. Naw. It's just coincidence."

"I don't know," said Sherman. "Indians don't believe in coincidence."

"Yeah, well, none of this had anything to do with me," said Jack.

"I hope you're right," said Sherman.

"But it did, too," said Maggie.

"What?" said Jack. "What do you mean?"

"It did have something to do with you. Don't you remember? You decided that Bob's strange behavior was related to his jealousy of you."

"Oh, yeah, but I can't see how that has any real or direct bearing on what happened up there. Or here. I can't see any connection, beyond the fact that that may be what had him acting so weird. And that's been going on for a few years."

"You be careful," said Sherman. "Keep your eyes open. Okay? I got to get back home now. Thanks for the coffee, Maggie."

Sherman was just turning out of the driveway when Maggie went into the kitchen and opened the refrigerator. She stood for a moment looking puzzled. Then she called out to Jackson.

"Jack," she said. "Come here."

Jack stepped back into the kitchen.

"What is it, babe?" he said.

"Somebody's been into our food."

Sherman Postoak fought his GMC pickup along a narrow and unpaved road scored by deep ruts made when the road was wet and hardened with drying. The road wound its way with sharp curves through thick and tangled woods, all the while climbing higher and higher into the foothills of the Ozark Mountains. A sudden curve revealed almost at once a scene shocking by its contrast to its surroundings. There was a wide open expanse of well-kept yard with a new house of the variety known in those parts as Indian house. A new and modern home built by the Housing Authority of the Cherokee Nation of Oklahoma, it was expansive and brick-fronted. A ten-year-old Dodge was parked to one side of the house, and off to the other side stood a small, solidly constructed frame building. The small house was unpainted and still had the look of new lumber.

In front of the small house stood an old Indian man. He was small with a slight stature, and he wore a dark blue plaid shirt with baggy khaki trousers. His hair was still black and was cut short. He appeared to be waiting for someone, and as Sherman pulled his pickup into the old man's yard, he smiled, a smile that not only indicated that he was pleased to have a visitor but also that he was pleased with himself. Sherman interpreted that smile and the twinkle in the old man's eye in the following way: *He knew I was coming. He's been just standing there waiting for me, because he knew I was coming, even though I didn't call ahead or send word or anything like that. He just knew it.*

Sherman parked and got out of his pickup. He approached the old one.

" 'Siyo," he said.

The old man responded in Cherokee. "Hello, Postoak. How are you?"

"I'm well, thank you," said Sherman, also in Cherokee. He extended his right hand and the old man responded in kind. They shook hands the traditional Cherokee way—soft—a handshake that would be interpreted by a white man as weak but in reality is simply not aggressively forceful. "And you? How are you?"

"I'm healthy for an old man. What brings you to see me? A visit?"

"No. Although I'm always glad for a chance to

visit with you, I came here today because I need your services."

"Come in," said the old man, and he opened the door to the small house and went inside. It was only one room with a front door and a back door. There were no windows. Several folding chairs were available in the room, and, other than that, it was furnished with one easy chair in which the old man sat, an ashtray on a stand beside the easy chair and a couple of plain wooden tables. One was covered with a variety of samples of plant life. The other was bare and empty save one corner, which held half a dozen clean, wooden bowls of various sizes and some sticks. Plants and herbs hung drying all along the walls. On the stand beside the chair was, in addition to the ashtray, a Cherokee-language Bible. The old man in his easy chair sat facing the front wall. He gestured to a folding chair to his right. Sherman sat down. He was not facing the old man, but rather the wall to the old man's left. The old man took out a cigarette and lit it.

"What can I do for you?" he said.

"It's that some very good friends of mine may be in trouble. If they are, I want to help them, and that may put me in trouble, too. I want something to protect me and my friends."

"What kind of trouble, Sherman?"

Sherman then told the old man what he could of the misadventures of the Wilders in Wyoming from what they had told him. There had been a disappearance and a killing, and they seemed somehow to be involved. Then he told the old man about the prowler he, himself, had encountered at the Wilders' house.

"I'm afraid that it is not over yet," he said.

The old man sat and puffed his cigarette. He smoked it down to the end, dropped it into the ashtray, and took out a new one. He picked up a wooden kitchen match, struck it on his shoe, and lit the cigarette.

"Are your friends Indian or white?" he asked.

"My friend Jack is Indian," said Sherman, "although he is part white. He's a mixed-blood. His wife is a white woman."

"And these people who are trying to hurt them —are they Indian or white?"

"I think that they are all white people. But I really don't know who it is."

"Can you stay with me awhile?"

"Yes."

"Good," said the old man. "We'll fix some tobacco."

He finished smoking his second cigarette, got up from his easy chair and went to get a wooden bowl from the table. Then he sat down and reached for a can of Prince Albert smoking tobacco. He opened the can and poured the tobacco into the bowl.

Ajax jumped to the top of the old cast-off swamp box window unit air conditioner that stood on the inside of the fence in the tall grass. He liked it for its height. He pranced on it, his hooves clicking against the tin. He surveyed his world, including that forbidden part on the other side of the fence—that part where the people moved freely in and out, back and forth, that part where the grass tasted so much sweeter. He looked longingly at the fence. He was high enough to jump it easily, but he was much too far away, and he knew it. Yet he looked and he thought about it.

He bleated and his bleat was answered. Crackerjacks came through the tall weeds, not much showing her condition yet, and stood beside the swamp box. Ajax did not look down to acknowledge her presence, yet he was pleased that she was there. Crackerjacks was shy of people and spent her time, when they were around, back in the weeds or in the woods or inside the small barn.

Suddenly there was a sound from back in the woods—the crunching of dried leaves, a rustling of the weeds. Crackerjacks disappeared with two long bounds into the tall weeds in the opposite direction from whence the sound had come. Ajax stamped around on the tin box and turned to face the noise. He was not so timid as was his little sister—or mate. He did not fear man. He made use of man. He manipulated man. He waited, his head held high, his ears pricked forward. His chest swelled with pride and arrogance and conceit. Then he saw the figure of the man emerge from the woods, moving toward him. He waited with anticipation as the man came closer. Suddenly Ajax stiffened. He did not know this man. He bleated. He vaulted from the swamp box into the tall weeds and vanished in the still fresh wake of Crackerjacks.

Inside the house Jack and Maggie had just finished eating the Dairy Queen hamburgers that Jack had driven into town for. The grocery supply in the house was somewhat depleted, due to a combination of planning before the trip and of the mysterious visitor to their house in their absence, and neither of them felt like a shopping trip just yet. Jack stuffed the napkins and the burger wrappings into the bag he had brought the stuff home in, wadded it all up and crossed the kitchen floor to dump it in the trash. He wiped at his mouth with a shirt sleeve.

"Well," he said, "what do you think, babe?"

"What do I think? About what?"

"About your lecherous and lascivious goat out there?"

"Oh."

"Now this is serious. He's carried on badly out there with his own sister and he's got her pregnant. What are we going to do?"

"Don't be silly. We're not going to do anything."

"Maybe we should get her an abortion."

"Jack."

"That way no one would ever find out. She'd be spared all that public scorn, humiliation, disgrace. Reproachful, opprobrious looks."

Maggie leaned her elbows on the table and put on a pensive look.

"Maybe you're right," she said, "but where could we take her? Do you think that Dr. Hill would perform an abortion?"

"I don't know," said Jack. "Doc Hill is awfully conscious of public opinion, you know. I'm afraid he'd knuckle under the pressure of the local antiabortion interests."

"Then where can we take her?"

"Juarez," said Jack. "That's where we'll go. Juarez. No one around here will ever know."

"Well," said Maggie, "you'll have to ask Sherman to watch the house again."

"Oh, he'll do it. No problem. I'll take care of it right away."

There was a noise outside, followed by the clear sound of footsteps on the porch. Both Wilders stopped talking and looked toward the front door, then at each other. Usually they would hear a car drive up before anyone came to their door. Then there was a knock.

"I didn't hear anyone drive up," said Jack. "Did you?"

"No," said Maggie.

Jack got up and went to the door. Maggie sat tense at the table. The recent events in Wyoming and at their home in Oklahoma had them both edgy and apprehensive. At the door Jack hesitated for an instant. He wished that the screen door had been latched so that he could feel a bit safer in opening the other. He put his hand on the knob, turned it and pulled the door open, a bit too quickly. His heart thumped in his chest. He stood dumbfounded.

"Hello, Jack, old buddy. Ain't you going to invite me in?"

"Bob Drago," said Jack. "What the hell are you doing here?"

Chapter Nine

PUDGE EVANS HAD just walked into his office when the phone call came. It was the New York City policeman he had talked to several days earlier when he had called for information on Bob Drago and Leland Krakes. It was a Captain Wellman. Pudge was surprised to hear from the man.

"Sheriff Evans, the reason I'm calling is that I've got some new information on your missing person, Robert Drago. Is your case still open?"

"Yes, it is," said Pudge, "and I hope you've got something good, because it don't look any more promising now than it did when I last talked to you. What've you got?"

"You remember I told you that it didn't appear to us that Drago had spent any of the money he got out of his movie scam with those local investors?"

"Yeah. That's why Krakes was nosing around here. Trying to find the cash. At least that's what he said."

"Well," said Wellman, "he probably was. As far as we can tell, those investors don't know anything. Drago took them to the cleaners. But I just talked to some boys in narcotics who tell me that Drago spent the dough—all of it—on some bad crack."

"I think I know what you're saying, Captain Wellman," said Pudge, "but I'm just an old country sheriff. Could you be a little bit more specific with me?"

"He bought what he thought was a hundred thousand dollars' worth of crack, probably thinking that he'd be able to turn it into a quarter of a million. The stuff was crack, all right, but it was a bad mixture. It's not worth a dime."

"Captain Wellman," said Pudge, "just what is crack?"

"It's a mixture of coke, you know, cocaine, and baking soda," said Wellman. "The latest thing. The most popular right now, too. Drago's problem was that he didn't know what the hell he was doing. I'd guess that this was his first attempt to get into this business. Somebody sold him a big batch of baking soda with a dime's worth of coke in it."

"Well, I'll be damned," said Pudge.

"Do you know any more about the whereabouts of Drago?"

"No, sir, I don't."

"Well, then, now you have two questions. Where is Drago, and where is the bad crack?"

"No, sir, Captain," said Pudge. "I've got three. We had a murder here since I last talked to you."

"Related?"

"It would seem to be. Captain Wellman, if your narcotics boys know so much about what Mr. Drago was up to, why didn't they place him under arrest instead of allowing him to run around all over the country?"

"Well, Sheriff, you got to understand how those guys work. They get out in the streets and they work undercover. They spend weeks, months, setting up a bust. The thing is, they know a lot of stuff about what's going on out there, but they don't always have the evidence to make a good case. So they just keep watching. In the Drago case, they tell me, it wouldn't have been worth busting Drago. A bust at that time would have blown a much bigger case they were working on. Drago and his bad crack just wasn't worth taking the chance."

"And as a result I've got a missing person, two men in jail and an unsolved murder on my hands out here in Wyoming."

"That's the breaks. Say. I do have one other bit of information I can pass along to you that might be related to your case."

"Well, let me have it," said Pudge.

"The boys in narcotics told me they've been watching two other men. These guys are acquainted with Drago. They're in the same line of work. They're all writers. What's more, they all have the same agent. These two, they tell me, are definitely into the drug business. They're not real big time, but they're into it. They know what they're doing. We don't have anything to connect Drago's bad buy with these two, but like I said, they're all well acquainted with each other. It's a hell of a coincidence if that's all it is. By the way, we've lost them, too, but the word is they might be headed for Oklahoma."

"Oklahoma?" said Pudge. "What are their names?"

"John Garretson and Vaughan Hacker."

"Damn," said Pudge.

"What is it?"

"They were just here. Both of them. Captain Wellman, I don't know about your big-city investigations, but I'd dearly appreciate it if you'd give me a call if you hear or see anything of those two again. As of right now, they're wanted for questioning regarding a murder by the state of Wyoming."

"Sheriff, we try to cooperate every way we can."

"Well," said Pudge, "I appreciate that. Thanks for the call."

He hung up the phone and roared out at the top of his voice.

"George."

George was standing in the doorway to Pudge's office in a matter of a few seconds.

"Yes, sir?"

"George, you got them names and addresses and phone numbers from out at the ranch?"

"Yes, sir."

"See if you can get ahold of Jack Wilder right away quick."

"He's back in Oklahoma, Sheriff."

"I know that. You know how to dial long distance?"

"Yes sir," said George, and he vanished even more quickly than he had appeared.

Pudge leaned back in his chair with a long sigh.

"Dammit," he said out loud, though there was no one in his office to hear.

The Beechcraft Bonanza equipped with special floats was cruising at 130 knots at an altitude just under three thousand feet. No flight plan had been filed, and it flew low to avoid radar detection. The VOR was useless at that altitude, so John Garretson relied on his knowledge of the terrain, which was minimal, and frequent glances at the ADF and the loran. In the seat beside him, Vaughan Hacker appeared nervous. He studied the instruments, though they meant nothing to him, and he kept looking back behind him at the briefcase on the empty seat as if it might have gone somewhere. He knew that was foolish under the circumstances, but a quarter of a million dollars was a lot of money. He spoke to Garretson through the David Clark headsets they wore.

"John," he said, "do you really think that little bastard will be there?"

"He'll be there."

"How do you know? He's a goddamn drunk."

"What we've got in that briefcase back there is enough to sober anybody up. He needs the bread. Okay?"

"What if he tries to pull something on us? What if he hasn't even got the stuff and he's trying to pull a fast one?"

"He's too big a chicken to try anything like that," said Garretson, beginning to get impatient with the conversation. "Just calm down, will you? You're making me nervous, and I've got to fly this thing. Think of the profit we'll make on this deal."

The sun was low on the horizon, and Vaughan Hacker looked at his wristwatch.

"Are we going to make it on time?" he asked.

"We're doing fine, Vaughan. Just fine. We're going to be right on time. Okay?"

"I don't know, man. Nothing's gone right on this deal. I don't like it. You had to go and kill that crazy old cook, and we're dealing with a drunk. I don't like it."

"Just take it easy, I said. Everything will be all right if you don't blow your cool. All right?"

"I don't know why we had to set this deal up all the way down to Oklahoma," said Hacker. "Oklahoma. Damn."

"That's the way Drago wanted it."

"Oklahoma," said Hacker, and he glanced back over the seat again at the briefcase.

Jack Wilder stepped back from the door and held his hands out to his sides in a gesture of futility. He did not open the screen door for Bob Drago. Drago opened it himself and stepped inside. He was wearing the same suit he had last been seen in at the Hunter Ranch. He looked bedraggled and disarranged. He was in need of a shave, and his hair was generally tousled. Tiny burrs that Jack had known all his life but never had a name for covered the rumpled and dirty suit.

"That's not much of a welcome for an old friend you haven't seen in seven years," said Drago. "I expected a little better from you."

"It hasn't been seven years, Bob," said Jack. "It's been less than a week."

Drago scratched his head.

"Yeah," he said, "I guess I did see you up there. I wasn't sure. I was, uh, kind of messed up that night. Sorry."

Just then Maggie stepped in from the kitchen.

"Bob?" she said.

"Oh, hi, Maggie. I, uh, I was just reminded by Jack that I saw you guys in Wyoming. I guess I should apologize for the condition I was in that night. I hope I didn't say anything I shouldn't have. Is that what's wrong, Jack? Did I say something wrong? Forget it, man. It was the booze talking. Hey. It's me. Bob Drago. Remember?"

"Yeah," said Jack. "I remember."

"Well, come on, then. What's this cold-shoulder routine? Huh?"

"Bob, look at yourself. What the hell are you up to?"

Jack indicated a mirror on the living-room wall, and Drago stepped over before it. He looked in at the wretched-looking image he presented, shrugged his shoulders and smirked.

"I look pretty rugged, all right," he said. "I been walking through these damn woods to get here."

"How long have you been out there?" asked Jack.

"I don't know. Not long."

Maggie remembered the clothes that Bob Drago had worn when last she saw him in Wyoming. She thought about his disappearance and about his present state, then about the prowler Sherman had encountered and the missing food from her kitchen.

"Bob," she said, "did you come straight down here from the ranch? Have you been here all this time?"

Drago hesitated.

"Come on, Bob," said Jack. "Just what the hell is going on here, huh?"

"Listen, Jack. Maggie," said Drago with a sudden and too sincere note to his voice, "I need your help. I need it real bad. You're the only friends I have left in the world. That's why I'm here."

Jack paced across the floor, rubbed his face, and paced back to where he had started from.

"Sit down, Bob," he said. "Sit down."

Drago sat in a chair with a rough fabric covering, and Maggie winced at the thought of the burrs catching in the fabric.

"Now," said Jack, "suppose you tell us what you've been up to. Why did you leave the ranch without telling anyone where you were going?"

"Why'd you leave all your things?" added Maggie.

"I just got sick of all those damn phonies," said Drago. "I had to get out."

"That's a bunch of crap, Bob," said Jack. "Look. We know about the hundred thousand dollars you swindled those people out of in New York. We know about that. They hired a private detective. He came out to Wyoming looking for you. Or looking for the money or something."

"A private detective? Are you sure?"

"Yeah, we're sure."

"I mean, the man might have been lying, you know? There are some guys after me. Gangsters from the city. I—I didn't tell you the whole truth. That's why I left the ranch in such a hurry. Something happened. I thought they were there."

"The arrow in the wall?" said Maggie.

"Yeah. That's right. I thought they were there and figured I'd better get out. I came here to hide. I didn't think you'd mind if I used your place for a short time. We're old friends. Aren't we?"

"We used to be friends, Bob," said Jack. "Do you have any idea what you put us through? Hell, man, we thought you'd been murdered."

"I'm sorry about that, Jack. I really am, but when those guys from the city shot that arrow at me, I just didn't think. I got out fast. I was scared. Then I couldn't think of a safe place to go, so I came here."

"It was Will McCarty who shot the arrow," said Jack.

"Will McCarty?"

"Will McCarty, and he did it because you'd poured a drink all over him. That's all. No gangsters. Just Will."

"I'll be damned."

"You probably will be if there's any justice in the universe."

"But you said there was a detective. Right? You see, they are after me."

"Bob, we know someone's after you. You swindled them out of a lot of money. And listen to this. The cook, Sourdough, you remember him?"

"Yeah, I think so. I'm not sure."

"He's dead, Bob. He's dead because of you. He saw you talking to someone, he said suspiciously, and he was going to tell me who it was. He was murdered before he had a chance."

"Hey," said Drago, standing up and walking across the room, "I don't know anything about that. Don't try to lay that on me, Jackson. This is the first I heard anything about it."

"But it was because of you, Bob," said Maggie.

"Bob, you're in too deep," said Jack. "Whatever it is you're in, you're in it too deep. Now let us help you. Okay?"

"That's why I'm here," said Drago. "For your help."

"Okay. Now listen to me, Bob. We'll call the sheriff here in just a minute. He's a friend of mine. We can trust him to handle this thing the right way. You say that you didn't know anything about Sourdough. I believe you. You can give that money back to its rightful owners, and I think we can still get you out of this pretty easy. Okay? We'll call the sheriff. Maggie, give Glen Bird a call, will you, babe?"

"No," said Drago.

"Bob," said Maggie, "it makes sense."

"Just keep away from that phone."

"Now wait a minute," said Jack, but before he could go on, Bob Drago had pushed back the left side of his rumpled suit coat to reveal the handle of a Ruger target pistol. Jack recognized it and knew that it was a .22.

"No phone calls," said Drago.

"You threatening to shoot me?" said Jack. "My wife?"

"Hey," said Drago, "I just didn't want you to make a phone call. Okay? Come on. Sit back down and let's talk this over. Sit down."

Jack and Maggie sat down on the couch at opposite ends. Drago dropped back into the same chair he had been in before.

"You said you wanted my help, Bob," said Jack. "Our help. The only way I know to help is to call the sheriff and get this all straightened out. Let you get that money back where it belongs."

"I don't have the money," said Drago.

"Don't tell me that you spent a hundred thousand dollars already and nobody knows about it. What'd you spend it on? A hundred thousand."

"I didn't spend it exactly," said Drago. "I sort of invested it."

"What do you mean, 'sort of invested it'?"

"I bought some stuff that I can sell for a profit."

"What kind of stuff?"

"You don't need to know, Jack. All right? The less you know about this, the better off you'll be. Hell, buddy, I don't want to get you involved."

"It's a little late for that," said Jack.

"We've been involved in this since the night you disappeared," said Maggie. "We got ourselves involved because you were our friend. No one else seemed to be concerned, but you were our friend. Bob, did you wreck the jeep?"

Drago snickered.

"Yeah," he said. "I wanted to disappear and hide out long enough to get this deal made, so I thought that if I made it look like something had happened to me up there, maybe no one would be looking for me anywhere else. I ran the jeep off the road."

"What about the arrow with your blood type on it?" asked Jack. "Do you know about that? Did you do that, too?"

"I cut my arm on the damn jeep door when I ran it off the road," said Drago, and he turned his left arm slightly to show where the coat and shirt sleeves were torn. Blood still showed on the material, though it was not readily notice- able because of the general condition of his clothing. "Then I saw that arrow. It looked like the one that had been shot at me, so I picked it up and daubed it around on the wound."

"Then you carried it all the way out into the middle of that field?" said Jack.

"Yeah. I rode a horse across the field from where I left the jeep. I dropped off the arrow about halfway. At the highway I climbed over the fence and left."

"Somebody pick you up at the highway?" asked Jack.

"That's all you need to know, old buddy," said Drago. "Let's get back to the real business at hand. I need a ride."

"I told you," said Jack, "the only way I can help is to call the sheriff."

Drago pulled the Ruger out of his waistband and held it casually in front of him pointed at the back of the couch between Jack and Maggie.

"I hoped that it wouldn't have to come to this," he said.

"You'd kill us?" said Maggie.

"Don't make us find out," said Drago. "Okay? All we're going to do is to go for a ride. It's not too far from here. You just take me there, I make my sale and you can go home. You'll never see me again."

"Where's your merchandise?" said Jack.

"It's already in the back of your pickup. Get the keys and let's go," said Drago, looking at his watch. "It's just about time."

"What you got out there, Bob," said Jack, "drugs? You dealing drugs?"

"Shut up," said Drago. He leveled the Ruger at Jack. "Just get the keys."

Jack stood up and reached into the pocket of his jeans.

"I got them right here," he said. Then he looked at Maggie. "It's okay, babe," he said. "I'll be back in a little while. Right, Bob?"

"Maggie's going with us," said Drago. "Come on."

Pudge Evans sat behind his desk holding the telephone to his ear in his right hand. His left hand drummed the desk brutally. Finally he slammed the receiver back down on the hook and yelled.

"George."

"Yes, sir?"

George was already standing in the doorway to Pudge's office anticipating some order.

"George, get a map of Oklahoma or something. Find out what county Jack Wilder lives in. Then get ahold of the county sheriff. Be quick about it, too. Dammit, I think something's about to happen down there, and I think he might be in trouble."

"Right away, Sheriff," said George, and he rushed away to do his research.

"Dammit," said Pudge, and he pounded on his desk three times with his big left fist.

"Where are we going?" said Jack, as he pulled onto the highway.

Maggie sat next to him, and riding shotgun with his Ruger was Bob Drago.

"Lake Tenkiller," said Drago. "Cherokee Landing. Remember?"

"Yeah, I know the place. Who the hell you going to meet at Cherokee Landing?"

"Just never mind who," said Drago. "Couple of guys with a water plane are meeting me there. They're going to take this stuff out of your pickup and then they're going to give me a cool quarter of a million bucks. How's that sound to you, old buddy? A quarter of a million bucks."

"You'll never get away with this, Bob," said Jack.

"Hell, man, I'll be out of the country before anyone knows that I'm not lying dead up in Wyoming somewhere. You just drive."

"Bob?" said Maggie.

"What?"

"Bob, are you planning to kill us after we drive you out there?"

"No. Dammit, Maggie, I told you I'd let you go. I don't want to hurt you. I just need your help. I won't use this thing unless I have to."

"But your friends might not feel the same way you do," Maggie said. "From what I hear, when people buy or sell drugs they don't want to leave any witnesses behind to tell about it. Your friends will want to kill us."

"Look," said Drago, "we'll get there before they do. I've got this thing timed just right. We'll get there first, and I'll let you go before they get there. Okay?"

"So we can get back to a phone and bust up the whole deal?" said Jack. "No. I don't buy that. You're not that stupid."

"I'll let you go on foot. I'm keeping the pickup. By the time you get to a phone from Cherokee

Landing walking, I'll have my money and be long gone."

Jack realized that Drago was right. That would be possible. Still, he did not believe Drago. He was certain that either Drago or his accomplices, whoever they might be, would indeed try to kill him and his wife. He thought about trying to jump Drago before they arrived at the landing, but Maggie was between the two of them. Jack wasn't afraid of Drago, even with a gun. He realized that he might be foolish not to fear a man with a gun, but still he didn't fear Drago. Not for himself. But he was afraid. He was deathly afraid for the safety of Maggie, and then he realized that he was afraid for himself. He knew that if it were not for Maggie, he would be a man absolutely alone in this world, no matter what it might look like to anyone else. He would have his friends and acquaintances. He would still receive attention from the press and from his fans, from publishers and from others in the book industry. But without Maggie, he would be alone.

"You mean that, Bob?" he said. "You'll let us go before the plane shows up?"

"I promise, Jack."

An old GMC pickup came at them from the opposite direction on the two-lane road. Jack recognized it from a good distance away, but he showed no sign. He was glad that Maggie kept quiet, too. He casually dropped his left arm out the window and let it hang down by the door. When the GMC got closer, Sherman Postoak was clearly visible behind the wheel. Sherman saw Jack and Maggie, and he saw the man riding with them. He had a sudden glimpse in his mind of a face—a face to go with the body that had come rushing upon him so suddenly one day at the Wilders' house—the man who had knocked him backward onto the ground and then vanished into the woods. And it fit with a dim memory from the past. *Bob Drago,* he said to himself. He saw that Jack Wilder was deliberately avoiding looking at him, deliberately not acknowledging him with a wave or a nod as they passed on the highway. And then he saw the hand down by the door, twisted at the wrist and making strange gestures. It appeared to be trying to point back into the cab. At Drago? It made itself into a gun and tried to shoot. *He's trying to tell me that guy's got a gun. Is that what he's trying to tell me?* All this took place in an instant, and the pickups had passed on the road. Sherman watched in his rear-view mirror until he could no longer see the Ford. *Where's he going? The man's got a gun.* He eased his foot up off the gas pedal and pulled off the highway into the overgrown weeds on the shoulder. Turning around in the seat he looked after the Ford. It was completely out of sight. He knew that he had to follow, but he also knew that he couldn't allow Drago, if indeed that was Drago in there with Jack and Maggie, to know that he was being followed. He slipped the GMC's gearshift lever into first and started to ease back onto the road, but a line of cars came over the hill.

"Damn," he said.

He waited for the cars to pass on by, then he twisted the big pickup through a u-turn and pressed the pedal to the floor. He figured that if he drove fast enough, he'd be able to catch up to Jack before they came to any possible turning-off spot. He needed to get that Ford back in sight before the sun went down. He'd worry about what to do next when the time came.

"Is this Sheriff Glen Bird of Cherokee County, Oklahoma?" said Pudge Evans into his telephone.

"Yes, sir, this is Sheriff Bird talking. What can I do for you?"

"Sheriff Bird, this is Sheriff Pudge Evans calling. Sheridan County, Wyoming."

"Wyoming?"

"That's right," said Pudge. "Sheriff, do you know a man in your county by the name of Jackson Wilder?"

"Jack Wilder? Sure. Everybody knows Jack. He's a famous writer. Writes western books. Good ones, too. I just read one last week."

"Yes, I know," said Pudge, not trying too hard to hide his impatience. "I, too, know Mr. Wilder. Do you know where he lives?"

"Yeah, I been out to his place before. It ain't too far from here."

"Could you go out there or send somebody out there to check on the Wilders? I've tried to call them and nobody answers the phone. I have reason to believe that Jack Wilder may be in danger."

"Jack? What kind of danger?"

"Sheriff Bird, I don't know if I have time to explain all of this to you."

"All right then," said Bird, "hold the phone. I'll send someone right out there, and then I'll get back on the line, and you can tell me all about it. Okay?"

"Yes. Please hurry."

Bird put down his phone.

"Jerry," he said.

Across the room a young deputy with his feet on a desk sat reading a copy of *Playboy*. He looked up from the centerfold.

"Yeah?"

"Jerry, you know where Jack Wilder lives, don't you?"

"Yeah."

"Well, take a drive out there and see if everything's all right."

"Now?"

"Right now. Get going."

The deputy tossed down the *Playboy* and started toward the door.

"Don't fool around on the way either," shouted the sheriff as the young man went out the door. Bird went back to the phone on his desk.

"All right, Sheriff Evans," he said. "I've got a man on the way out there right now. Can you tell me what this is all about?"

Pudge filled Sheriff Bird in on the gathering of Tom Brock's clients at the Hunter Dude Ranch near Sheridan. He told him of the disappearance of Robert Drago and all the mysterious and possibly related occurrences. And he told him of the latest phone call he had received from the New York City police.

"What it looks like, Sheriff Bird," said Pudge, "is that Drago may still be alive and kicking, and that he may be trying to sell this bad batch of crack he bought to someone else. We don't know where he's at. But New York thinks that them other two might be headed your way. I've just had another call from up there. I don't know how they find these things out, but they tell me that they think Garretson and Hacker are headed for Oklahoma. And there's one other thing. This John Garretson is a licensed pilot. He could be flying in."

"Well, Sheriff," said Bird, "that ain't much to go on. You want me to call you back when my man gets back from Jack's place?"

"I sure do," said Pudge. "Right away as soon as you know anything. If you get hold of Jack Wilder, I'd like to talk to him, too."

Sherman Postoak caught up with the Ford before it reached Tahlequah. He was glad of that, because Jack could have turned in any one of a number of directions once he got there. What he did was turn right on Highway 62 and head out of town toward Muskogee. *Where the hell are they going?* Sherman asked himself. He followed the Ford on through town and out toward the Cherokee Nation's tribal complex, but he was careful to allow some traffic to get between himself and the pickup he was following. Just before they reached the tribal complex, Jack Wilder turned left onto Highway 82 which would take him to Keys and Cookson if he went that far. If he went farther than that, it would take him on out to Lake Tenkiller. Sherman slowed his GMC down. He didn't want Drago—he was pretty sure by this time that the man with Jack and Maggie was in fact Drago—to notice that they were being followed. He allowed a couple of cars to pass him on the narrow highway. They drove straight through Keys, past the sign that advertised Big Red's café, open all night, "in the heart of the financial district of downtown Keys, Oklahoma." They drove on. In Cookson, Sherman pulled off the highway and into the parking lot of the Dairy Prince Drive-In at the edge of town. He left his engine running and ran inside to the pay telephone. Fumbling in his pocket, he found the right change and dropped it in the slot. He flipped through the worn and ragged pages of the book there on the shelf and found a number, then punched the buttons on the phone.

"Hello," he said, "let me talk to Sheriff Bird."

"This is Bird talking."

"Glen, this is Sherman Postoak."

"Well, hi, Sherman. What's going on?"

"Glen, I'm in a hurry. I'm trying to follow Jack Wilder and Maggie in their pickup."

"What?"

"Listen, Glen. I think they're in trouble."

"You, too. Where are they?"

"I'm at the Dairy Prince in Cookson. Just stopped to call. They're on ahead of me on Eighty-two. I don't know where they're going."

"You keep after them, Sherm. I'll get out there as fast as I can and try to find you all."

A mile or so outside of Cookson on the other side, Jack Wilder turned right onto a dirt road that wound through thick woods. He could remember many a time in years now long past he and Drago had driven this same road together, sometimes just the two of them, sometimes with their wives. It was a favorite spot of theirs back in those days, for fishing, for swimming, for a picnic, or just for sitting quietly and talking. Jack resented Drago's using the spot now for his drug deal. He drove on in silence.

"Hey," said Drago as they came to the end of the road where the trees just seemed to open up on a broad expanse of beach with the wide lake on farther out in front of them. "Hey, pull up close to the trees here."

Jack stopped the pickup at the edge of the woods. No one was in sight. Drago looked at his watch.

"Any minute now," he said.

"Can we go, then?" said Maggie.

"Not yet. Just hold on. I'll let you know. Get out. Go on, get out."

Drago had opened the passenger-side door and stepped out into the sand. He gestured at Jack and Maggie with his Ruger. Jack opened the door on the driver's side and stepped out, then gave a hand to Maggie, who followed him. Keeping his pistol aimed generally at the Wilders, Drago wandered toward the water. As he walked, he looked up into the sky.

"You hear anything?" he said.

"Nothing," said Jack.

"Wait. Shut up. Listen."

The sound of a small plane came down from the sky, and Drago ran up and down the beach looking in all directions.

"There. There it is," he said. "I'm a rich man, Jackson, old buddy. A rich man."

The Beechcraft Bonanza came closer, and Drago waved frantically at it.

"Turn on the lights," he shouted.

"What?" said Jack.

"The lights on your pickup. Turn them on. Hurry up."

Jack reached inside the cab and pulled the lights on as the plane circled above them. It made a swing out over the lake, then slowly descended and came to a smooth, gliding stop on the water. The door of the plane opened.

"That you, Drago?" came a voice from the plane.

"Over here," shouted Drago. "Yeah. It's me. Come on over."

Jack took Maggie by the arm and moved slowly toward the pickup. The moon was bright in the sky, and it seemed that the night offered no cover. Drago looked around just as Jack was about to open the door.

"Hey," he shouted, aiming the Ruger at Jack, "get away from there. Move out this way. Come on."

John Garretson had jumped out of the plane and was running through the shallow water toward the beach.

"Who the hell have you got with you?" he shouted.

"It's all right," said Drago. "I'll get rid of them."

"Who is it?"

Garretson had made his way up to Drago and was looking toward Jack and Maggie, but they were between him and the lights of the pickup.

"John Garretson," said Jack. "Well, I'll be damned."

Garretson squinted and stepped closer to Jack.

"Jack Wilder?" he said. "And Maggie?"

"That's right, John," said Jackson.

Garretson turned on Drago.

"You damn fool," he said.

"Hey," said Drago, "I had to get out here some way, didn't I? They drove me. I'll take care of it."

"Damn right you will," said Garretson. "Where's the stuff?"

"Where's my money?" said Drago.

"The money's in the plane. When I see the stuff, I'll get it for you."

"Two hundred and fifty thousand?" said Drago.

"That's what we agreed on. A quarter of a million."

"The stuff is right there in the back of the pickup."

Garretson looked toward the pickup.

"You stay here and keep an eye on these two," he said, and he headed for the Ford.

"Well, hurry it up," said Drago. He had a hard time keeping his eye on the Wilders. He was too anxious for Garretson's response to the crack and for his payoff to follow. He looked from the Wilders to the pickup and then to the plane that contained his money. Garretson reached over the side of the pickup with a penknife, cut a slit in a package and dipped a finger into the white powder. He tasted it.

"Drago," he shouted. "Damn you. What are you trying to pull on me?"

"What? What are you talking about? Did you find it?"

Drago, forgetting his charge, ran toward the pickup. Jack grabbed Maggie by the arm.

"Come on," he said, and he ran toward the safety of the woods. In the plane Vaughan

Hacker could see that something was going wrong. He wished that he could fly. He was helpless in the plane—just sitting there. He reached under his jacket and pulled out a .45 automatic, jumped into the water and ran for the beach.

"Stop those two," he shouted. He fired two shots in the general direction of the woods into which Jack and Maggie had run. Garretson pulled a gun out of the waistband of his trousers and turned toward the commotion.

"Hold it," said Drago. "What about this stuff?"

"This stuff is worthless," said Garretson. "Right now we've got to get Jack and Maggie. Come on."

Garretson ran to join Hacker in his pursuit of the Wilders, and Drago saw his opportunity. He ran for the plane. Holding his Ruger up high, he ran through the shallow water until he reached the plane, then he climbed inside. He spotted the briefcase right away, opened it and saw the money.

"Damn," he said, and he snapped the briefcase closed again and, grabbing it up in his free hand, jumped back out of the plane. Hacker and Garretson were at the edge of the woods, undecided whether or not to pursue their quarry into the dark tangle.

"Let them go," said Garretson. "Let's get out of here."

Hacker turned to obey and saw Drago coming through the water with the briefcase.

"Look," he said.

Garretson turned and raised his pistol to aim at Drago, but before he could squeeze the trigger, Jack Wilder stepped out of the edge of the woods.

"Bob," he shouted. "Watch out."

Garretson pulled the trigger, and Bob Drago flew backwards into the water, still clutching the briefcase. The bullet had smashed his sternum. He was dead. At the same instant, Vaughan Hacker had turned toward Jack's voice and raised his pistol, but he didn't get a chance to fire. From within the dark bramble, Sherman Postoak raised his head, the cane pole at his lips. He expelled a sharp breath, and Hacker let out a scream of pain. The small locust-wood dart was embedded in the side of his neck. Sherman had the blowgun loaded again in an instant, and an instant later he had fired again. This time the dart struck Hacker in the middle of his back. Garretson had no idea what was getting Hacker, but the scene was suddenly too weird for him. The crack was no good. The money was floating in the water. And Hacker was screaming around on the beach. Garretson just wanted out. He ran toward where Drago's body floated in the shallow water still clutching the briefcase.

Suddenly, the air was filled with the sound of roaring engines and the night was lighted by the headlights of three cars, which came bounding onto the beach. Jack grabbed Maggie and pulled her back into the shadows. Sherman Postoak had already faded into the woods. Hacker had pulled the first dart out of his neck and was running after Garretson. He turned to face the new invasion and raised his pistol just as six car doors flew open and men came out of all of them.

"Hold it," shouted Glen Bird, his service revolver held out before him.

Hacker fired in panic, and his shot ricocheted off the sheriff's car. Bird pulled his trigger and sent a bullet into Hacker's chest. Hacker went over backward into the sand, his mouth and eyes wide open. He did not move again.

Out in the water, John Garretson had wrenched the briefcase from the dead grasp of Bob Drago, and he turned and fired three shots at the men on the beach. Then he ran for the plane. Throwing the briefcase ahead of him, he jumped in and started the engine. The plane began to move on the water. Ashore a man in a dark blue business suit with a neatly tied necktie stood spraddle-legged in the sand and held a .44 magnum out at arm's length before him in both hands. He pulled the trigger and the magnum roared. An instant later, the Beechcraft Bonanza flew to pieces in a deafening blast that seemed to rock the beach, and the flames that it shot forth reddened the lake and the night sky.

The shooter still held his weapon at the ready and looked menacingly around himself. The sheriff had by this time holstered his own revolver and had walked over to check on the man he had shot. He found him dead. Then he looked around the beach. He recognized the pickup of Jack Wilder.

"Jack," he shouted. "You out there? Jack Wilder?"

"Right over here," said Jack, and he stepped with Maggie out of the shadows of the woods. Sherman Postoak followed from another part of the trees that lined the beach. The three of them walked over to meet the sheriff.

"Jack, Maggie," said Glen Bird. "Are you two all right?"

"Yeah, Glen," said Jack, "everything's fine now. Who are all these guys?"

"OSBI," said Bird. "I had to call them in because of the drugs."

The agent for the Oklahoma State Bureau of Investigation, the one in the dark suit who had caused the explosion, just then came over to join the sheriff. He was returning his huge pistol to a shoulder holster and making quite an act of it.

"These the Wilders?" he asked.

"Yeah," said Bird. "Jack and Maggie Wilder. This is Sherman Postoak."

"I'm Agent Van Camp," said the man with the magnum. "OSBI."

"I'm pleased to meet you, Agent Van Camp," said Maggie.

"Yeah," said Jack, "we're, uh, glad you came."

"Were there just the two of them?" asked Van Camp.

"Bob Drago's out there in the water," said Jack. "Garretson shot him before you got here."

"Garretson?"

"He's the one you sent off in a blaze of glory."

"Oh."

"Jack," said Bird, "Van Camp will take over from here. I'm sure he'll want to get statements from all of you."

"Yeah, sure," said Jack, "but tell me something. How the hell did everybody wind up out here just in the nick of time? Can you tell me that?"

"Well," said Bird, "a sheriff up in Wyoming called me all worried about you, but mainly your good buddy, Sherman, here, was watching out for you. He followed you all the way out here, but he stopped off in Cookson long enough to call me. I called Van Camp and we hustled on out here. We radioed ahead and had the Lake Area Security Patrol watching, and they let us know which road Sherman turned off on. When we came down that road I seen his pickup pulled off to the side back there, so we knew we were on the right track."

"Well, I'll be damned," said Jack.

"Where's the crack?" said Van Camp.

"It's in the back of our pickup," said Maggie, pointing, "right over there."

Van Camp walked over to the pickup.

"Jack," said Sherman, "you got a cigarette?"

Jack slapped at his pockets.

"No," he said, "I, uh, must have lost them in all the excitement."

Sherman pulled his pack out of his shirt pocket and handed it to Jack.

"We'll smoke mine then," he said.

"Hey," Van Camp yelled from the pickup. "This crack's not even any good."

"Van Camp," said Bird, "why don't we all meet at my office in the morning, and we'll fill you in on all the details. That okay with you?"

"Well, yeah, sure."

Jack lit a cigarette and handed the pack back to Sherman. Sherman took one out and lit it.

"Just one, buddy," said Jack. "We've got to get back home and check on that old goat."

A Message To Our Readers...

As a person who reads books, you have access to countless possibilities for information and delight.

The world at your fingertips.

Millions of kids don't.

They don't because they can't read. Or won't. They've never found out how much fun reading can be. Many young people never open a book outside of school, much less finish one.

Think of what they're missing—all the books you loved as a child, all those you've enjoyed and learned from as an adult.

That's why there's RIF. For twenty years, Reading is Fundamental (RIF) has been helping community organizations help kids discover the fun of reading.

RIF's nationwide program of local projects makes it possible for young people to choose books that become theirs to keep. And, RIF activities motivate kids, so that they *want* to read.

To find out how RIF can help in your community or even in your own home, write to:

RIF
Dept. BK-2
Box 23444
Washington, D.C.
20026

Founded in 1966, RIF is a national nonprofit organization with local projects run by volunteers in every state of the union.

IF YOU HAVE A CASE FOR MYSTERY
— INVESTIGATE THIS FROM
PAGEANT BOOKS!

A HANA SHANER MYSTERY

...Now You Don't
Roma Greth

Set in the deceptively quiet Amish country, this
galvanizing thriller features a corpse that won't stay
dead. Remarkably shrewd Hana Shaner pieces
together a complex puzzle that paints a picture far
more sinister than a routine missing-persons
investigation.

ISBN: 0-517-00625-1   Price: $3.50

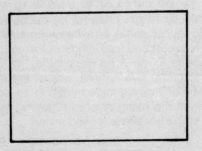

AVAILABLE AT BOOKSTORES NOW!

EVIL IS LURKING...

Jack Woods
WOLFFILE

Dr. Ian Sanders returns to his home off the coast of Maine for peace and tranquility. Instead he finds the island littered with bodies that have been clawed to death by a hairy, sub-human creature from whom the entire population is fleeing in fear. Will Dr. Sanders end the beast's ancient ritual of death or must he, too, become its victim?

0-517-00043-1 $3.50

ON SALE NOW
FROM PAGEANT BOOKS!